GHOSTS OF COUNTRY MUSIC

ABOUT THE AUTHOR

Matthew L. Swayne (State College, PA) is a journalist who currently works as a research writer at Penn State. He has done freelance reporting for major newspapers and other publications. This is Matt's third book. His first book, *America's Haunted Universities*, is a collection of tales about haunted colleges and universities.

GHOSTS OF COUNTRY MUSIC

TALES OF HAUNTED HONKY-TONKS & LEGENDARY SPECTRES

MATTHEW L. SWAYNE

Llewellyn Publications
Woodbury, Minnesota

First Edition
First Printing, 2017

Cover art: Dominick Finelle, The July Group
Cover design: Kevin R. Brown

Llewellyn Publications is a registered trademark of Llewellyn Worldwide Ltd.

Library of Congress Cataloging-in-Publication Data
Names: Swayne, Matthew L., author.
Title: Ghosts of country music : tales of haunted honky-tonks & legendary spectres / Matthew L. Swayne.
Description: First edition. | Woodbury, Minnesota : Llewellyn Publications, [2017] | Includes bibliographical references.
Identifiers: LCCN 2016044787 (print) | LCCN 2016051567 (ebook) (print) | LCCN 2016051567 (ebook) | ISBN 9780738748634 | ISBN 9780738751726 (ebook)
Subjects: LCSH: Haunted places. | Honky-tonk musicians. | Ghosts.
Classification: LCC BF1461.S925 2017 (print) | LCC BF1461 (ebook) | DDC 133.1--dc23
LC record available at https://lccn.loc.gov/2016044787

Llewellyn Publications
A Division of Llewellyn Worldwide Ltd.
2143 Wooddale Drive
Woodbury, MN 55125-2989
www.llewellyn.com

Printed in the United States of America

OTHER BOOKS BY MATTHEW L. SWAYNE

America's Haunted Universities

Haunted Rock & Roll

DEDICATION

Dedicated to my wife, Janice, who, over the past few years, was accidentally butt-dialed by a paranormal researcher on location, had her sleep disrupted dozens of times so that I could participate in radio shows at some God-forsaken hour, waited patiently at book signings, and withstood dozens of other inconveniences and annoyances without a complaint. Well, maybe not exactly without a complaint, but definitely far fewer complaints than I deserved.

CONTENTS

INTRODUCTION

For decades, people who have known and loved country music will tell you that there is something special about their music. Some say that the magic of country music arises from its purity and from the hearts and souls of country's singers and musicians. They create the spirit of the music that moves these fans like no other art form could.

Country music arose outside of the concrete jungles and factory yards, beyond the shadows of skyscrapers and shopping centers. Country musicians rarely attended prestigious music schools or took formal lessons in music theory—they felt the music instinctively. And their lives were immersed in music. When country music was just beginning to form out of the spiritual and popular styles of the day, music and dance was one of the primary forms of entertainment. It was played at parties and get-togethers. But it was more than just a form of entertainment. Most folk and country musicians, whether consciously or subconsciously, recognize music is transcendental. It played—and plays—a central role in worship services, for instance. Music rang out when people woke up, it surrounded them when they worked. They sang at happy occasions; they sang at sad events. They sang when loved ones died.

Of course, genetics may have played a role. The music that soared above the hills of Appalachia and echoed through the hollows has a texture that represented the Irish and Scottish roots of the folks who settled that rugged land. It was in their blood and in their bones. You might say it was in the souls of those people, too.

Eventually, these songs reached the ears of city people, who might not have known anything about the spirit-soothing nature of music but knew a thing or two about turning music into money. Cities—including Nashville, Knoxville, and Bristol, Tennessee; Branson, Missouri; and Shreveport, Louisiana—became music hubs, distributing the sweet, lonesome sounds of what was starting to be referred to as "country and western" music to places across the nation and around the world.

There's something else that traveled along with the twang of the banjos and strum of the guitars, something that proved country music was spirit-filled in more ways than one. Stories of spirits and ghosts came right along with the music: tales of witches and witch dances, and stories of ghost riders and demonic honky-tonkers. As some of the great practitioners of country music shuffled off both the musical and mortal stage, fans, friends, and family began to offer their own accounts of encounters with the spirits of these singers and pickers.

This wasn't a surprise for me. While researching my previous book, *Haunted Rock & Roll*, I realized that spirituality and rock music are deeply connected and this connection often reflects the culture of its musicians and fans. But it goes beyond rock music.

Music in itself is a spiritual act, one that involves every part of the musician and fan's being—body, mind, heart, and spirit.

In the following pages, I hope you will discover that the connections between song and spirit, music and mind are just as deep and just as true in country music. The same Irish, Scottish, and German settlers, who brought their folk tunes and melodies with them as they tamed the rugged Appalachian wilderness, also brought tales of ghosts and banshees, elves and fairies. Ghosts and witches, spooks and spirits also lie at the heart of Appalachian folklore. Are those beliefs and tales the reason for the long history of ghost stories in country music and country musicians? It's possible. In this book, we may not encounter an elf (but definitely an Elvis) or fairies, but we will read about ghosts of country musicians who continue to haunt mansions and recording studios.

We'll also read about ghosts that seem to stalk famous country stars. Loretta Lynn, the Coal Miner's Daughter, is easily one of country's most ghost-stalked stars. She is a sensitive soul whose contact with the supernatural goes back to her childhood in the coal mining region of Kentucky; however, Lynn's paranormal experiences became more frequent and more dramatic after she bought one of Tennessee's most haunted plantations, the site of tragedy, misfortune, and conflict.

There were others. Some of these country stars bought nightclubs that were plagued with supernatural activity and others played in haunted halls and spirit-filled stadiums. If you ask some fans and stars, several centers of country music—whole towns and cities, in fact—are haunted from city limit to city limit. We will visit those haunted locales, too.

So, that's all there is to it? Country music ghost stories are just superstitions mixed with fairy tales from the old country? Maybe not. Paranormal researchers and ghost hunters have been hot on the trail of these ghosts, and they offer evidence that spirits really do walk the halls of some of country and western music's most famous hangouts. These researchers usually conduct their investigations after receiving tips and leads from credible witnesses who have had spooky encounters with some of country music's biggest stars. We'll meet some of these ghost hunters ahead, as well as bring you accounts of people who have witnessed country music's supernatural side—and they tell us their encounters are not folklore or ghostlore; they witnessed real supernatural activity.

Just a few notes before we start. As with any business or home, haunted properties may change hands. Bars with a ghost or two lurking about may change owners, or, sadly, be torn down. Haunted houses may be sold. Country music stations with a paranormal past may change frequencies and formats, too.

Please remember, too, that many ghost stories remain an oral tradition. That means that often the exact details of the story do not jibe with historical events. I have tried to make those corrections, but some mistakes may still slide by. I apologize for those errors. Also, in order to hear some of these pieces of ghostlore, you often have to be in the location or part of that community where they occur. Despite my best efforts to tell every country music ghost story, I may have missed a ghost story about your cherished star or favorite haunted honky-tonk. It was unintentional. Please let me know if I did, though—this project was so much fun I'm always up for a sequel!

While I have tried to keep this material as contemporary, as all-encompassing, and as relevant as possible, these changes are inevitable.

It's equally important to note that some of the people who own these establishments may not mind a ghost hunter or ghost-hunting group investigating the property. Some of the spook-filled spots that I have encountered while researching this book even host tours. Others may not be so paranormal research–friendly. To add a third layer, some people who are happy to reveal their property's supernatural legacy may sell to new owners who want to maintain their privacy. If you are using this book as a guide to haunted properties in country music, please respect the privacy of owners and always ask permission before you begin a ghost-hunting adventure.

My father always said you should fear the living rather than the dead. I think he's right. The living, after all, have access to lawyers.

SECTION 1

THE GHOSTS OF COUNTRY MUSICIANS

In our first section, we'll look at stories of departed country stars who may not have completely left the stage, if you catch my drift. Ghosts of some of country's biggest stars and pioneers may continue to appear to friends, family, and fans long after their deaths. These spirits reportedly linger in sites that are connected with their lives and careers, such as their homes, clubs, and musical halls that were scenes of their greatest musical triumphs. Other tales in this section are about stars who are haunted—in other words, these are country stars who have had an encounter or a series of encounters with ghosts.

Some of the names that you'll read in the following pages might not surprise you. After all, it's not such a stretch to consider that the restless soul of Hank Williams may still be wandering the lonesome highways and visiting the clubs and bars that made him famous. But you may be surprised about the revelation that he is serving as a guardian angel—you read that correctly, Hank Williams a guardian angel—to geographically lost souls.

Here's another surprise: the ghosts of country musicians aren't relegated to the far past of the art form. In addition to Patsy and Hank, relatively new stars are adding their ghost stories to the mix.

First up, though, let's get ready to take a lonesome supernatural journey with arguably the greatest country star ever, Hank Williams.

CHAPTER 1

HANK WILLIAMS:
THE LONESOME
TRAVELER'S HAUNTED TRAIL

His songs were haunting.

His life was haunted.

His death was even more haunted.

There's no question that, if you asked fans who they would vote for as country music's most likely haunted entertainer of the year, it would be Hank Williams Sr.

One of the first real country superstars, Williams was born Hiram King Williams in Alabama. He started going by the name "Hank" when he set his sights on becoming a country performer as a teenager. He thought Hank sounded more country.

Once Williams started to write and record hit songs, he seemed almost unstoppable. In quick succession, he recorded songs that are listed as the most famous tunes in not just country music, but popular music, in general. "Honky Tonkin'," "Move It On Over," and "Lovesick Blues" were just a few in the string of hits that sailed into the top of the charts and assured his name—among other things—would be carried into immortality.

But fame and money didn't seem to settle Williams's restless soul. Biographers say that nagging back problems, in addition to other ailments, led to treatment with painkillers, and that treatment soon turned into an addiction. In the later stages of his career, Williams grew increasingly dependent on drugs and alcohol. His performances started to slide with this descent into drug and alcohol abuse. Williams was booted off of several radio programs and concert tours because he showed up late or showed up intoxicated or just didn't show up at all.

The career exile only accelerated the demise of the country superstar. His end finally came during a strange, but somehow fitting, car ride in West Virginia on New Year's Day 1953. The trip would turn into a country music legend. Williams hired a driver—a seventeen-year-old with the apt name for a chauffeur of Charles Carr—to take him from Montgomery, Alabama, to a scheduled show in Ohio. The 1,000-mile adventure quickly turned into a misadventure. Williams experienced back problems sitting in the car, so they decided to take a plane at Knoxville. The plane, however, turned back because of weather conditions, so the duo headed off to a hotel, just in time for the New Year's Eve celebration. After realizing that the musician and his driver were quickly falling behind schedule, Williams's nervous manager made them leave the hotel in the middle of the night. Williams was weak and coughing and had to be carried by bellboys into the car.

As Carr sped into the night and Williams slumbered silently, the driver had no idea the singer was experiencing health problems. The college freshman got a speeding ticket along the way and neither he, nor the officer, seemed to notice that Williams was ill. In Virginia, Carr asked Williams if he wanted something to eat, and the singer said he wasn't hungry. Those may have been his last words. It wasn't until Carr, who saw that the car was low on gas, pulled into a gas station in Oak Hill, West Virginia, that he realized Williams was dead.

The singer was just twenty-nine years old.

An autopsy was performed later and the official verdict was Williams died of heart problems and hemorrhage. As final as the coroner's inquest sounded, the Hank Williams mystery and his haunted legends were just beginning. It seemed that each location along Williams's famous death ride is now populated with ghosts.

In death, as in life, Williams's spirit keeps wandering. We'll take a look at some of the places where you might find the ghost of one of country music's most famous—and infamous—celebrities.

NASHVILLE

Back in the day, Hank Williams was the biggest headliner in Nashville, Tennessee, the cradle and, later, the epicenter for country and western music. Today, he still headlines. But now, he—or at least his ghost—is drawing in not just country fans but also paranormal investigators, ghost hunters, and people who just generally want to get the ever-loving crap scared out of themselves.

Williams's spirit is rumored to haunt several locations around the city. Some of the places we'll explore more deeply in future chapters, but for right now, we'll take a look at the major Music City centers for Hank hauntings. As you might expect, these sites are places that are integral to the history of country music.

Our first stop on the tour of Haunted Hank spots is at the Ryman Auditorium. As I'll cover in detail in the pages ahead, Ryman has an impressive haunted guest list, but Williams is, by far, the most popular. The Ryman, at the time of Williams's career, was the host site for the country's most popular radio show, the Grand Ole Opry. Williams played on the Grand Ole Opry numerous times.

Of the many spirits that continue to haunt this Nashville cultural treasure, Williams's spirit is said to be one of the most active. Witnesses say he continues to walk the halls of the Ryman, as well as perform on stage. Unlike many ghost stories at the Ryman that seem to be centered in a small area, Williams's ghost wanders all over the auditorium. He's been seen backstage, onstage, and everywhere in between.

Most say that the spirit of Hank Williams is behind one of the most famous haunted legends of the Ryman—usually just called the mist. People—mostly employees who spend an enormous amount of time in the Ryman long after the crowds have gone home—say they've encountered a cloudy form moving through the halls. The mist appears to know where it's going. All of the witnesses say there's no way they can predict when it's going to appear, or where they will see it.

So how do they know it's the ghost of Williams and not just, well, an amorphous, smoky cloud? Most of the witnesses suggest it's the feeling that accompanies the sighting. You just feel that it's Hank, they say.

But there's at least one story that confirms that the foggy phantasm is Hank Williams. The story goes like this: One night, an employee noticed something strange while making her rounds at the Ryman. She saw a misty cloud hovering onstage. Probably familiar with the tales of a misty apparition that haunted the Ryman, the staff member went closer to investigate. With each step that she took, the mist began to change appearance. The chaotic, smoky white form gradually turned into a more human shape. Displaying bravery that most of us would admire, but not imitate, the employee moved even closer and the human shape continued to transform. Now, she recognized that the ghost was taking the unmistakable thin, lanky form of Hank Williams, hunched over the microphone, almost like he was belting out one of his tunes, although there's no indication that the employee heard what song Hank was performing.

By the way, when the Grand Ole Opry transferred its operations from the Ryman into a more spacious, more modern facility in Opryland, a bunch of the theater's ghosts may have gone along for the ride, something we will discuss in an upcoming chapter. In fact, Hank's ghost may have gone along for the upgrade, too. People have detected his spirit at the new place, even though Hank seems to like appearing more often to the smaller, more intimate crowd in the Ryman.

MONTGOMERY

Montgomery, Alabama, was the big city for Williams as he grew up in the state's rural Butler County. The city would play an important part in the Hank Williams legend and, even today, is the sacred center for fans seeking to trace Williams's journey from a poor kid with a musical gift in Butler County to a songsmith learning his craft from street musicians in Greenville and Montgomery, Alabama, to eventual superstardom. As a poignant reminder of this connection with the city, Montgomery is both where Williams is buried and home to the Hank Williams Museum.

But some people say you can feel the singer's connection in other ways. One place that at least some people believe that the spirit of Williams has drifted into is a restaurant called Nobles, a restaurant in Montgomery, Alabama. It was once known as The Elite Lounge Casino Cafe and has the distinction of being the last place that Williams performed publicly.

Williams played a few songs for a meeting of a songwriter's association before heading off to his ill-fated car ride to West Virginia. By this time in Williams's career, he was still respected as a songwriter and still loved as a performer, but his drug and alcohol abuse caused his career to nosedive. The singer was often too intoxicated to perform or showed up late, causing television and radio producers, along with concert promoters, to avoid dealing with him.

Among his colleagues at the Elite, though, Williams appeared to be at home. He must have liked the reception at the Elite well enough because there are indications that he never left the restaurant in Montgomery and maybe even joined other spirits who reportedly haunt what was once one of the most popular clubs there.

Even before Williams's death people had said the place was paranormally active. Witnesses reported seeing a filmy fog drift through the restaurant, but it didn't seem to follow a draft or wind current; it seemed to have a mind of its own, navigating through the seating and halls. Other people encountered phenomena that defied their best attempts at a rational explanation. Reports indicate that there are more than filmy fogs and fleeting shapes that people have seen wafting through the rooms; they see actual shapes of people. They may not look quite solid, but these witnesses say these forms have a definite shape—a human shape.

It's the feeling that overwhelms customers and employees enough that they become convinced that the restaurant is haunted—and that Williams may be among the spirits that linger. One spirit, nicknamed "the man in the suit," has been seen at the restaurant. For fans of Williams, who was known to sport suits on stage, the description of this well-dressed spirit comes closest to their singing idol.

Williams was known to get a little out of hand every once in a while. At least one spirit—or spirits, and we'll get to that in a second—has been known to get feisty, too. There have been reports of loud noises and rappings. At other times, witnesses have watched as objects move on their own. People leave the room for a moment and when they return silverware is out of place and dishes have moved. For some of those visiting the restaurant, the displays are dramatic—chairs and tables move right in front of their disbelieving eyes.

During one visit by a group of ghost hunters, the team of investigators and restaurant guests went from room to room seeking to make contact with the resident spirit entities. In some cases, ghosts that inhabit a certain site are called *resident spirits*, not to be confused with *residual spirits* that are a paranormal phenomenon that features certain behaviors or activities that are repeated over and over again.

As the team entered the dining room, they tried to connect with a spirit with whom a psychic team member—Alabama-based Shawn Sellers, an author, medium, and paranormal researcher— believed he had contacted. As they called out to the spirit, a loud bang broke the session. They rushed to see what happened. A chair—which was a good three or four feet from the nearest member of the group—had flipped on its side.

"It was one of the craziest things I've ever seen," Sellers said. "I have never seen anything like it before and I can't explain it."

Was it a signal? Or a warning?

Often, though, the paranormal activity in the restaurant is more subtle than the chair-pitching ghost. People often say they feel like someone is watching them when they are in the restaurant. In fact, the feeling that a presence is near them follows guests and staff from room to room.

The main question, though, is: "Is it Hank?"

Possibly. But no one is exactly sure. The ghost hunters detected several presences in the restaurant. They felt that at least two were—for lack of a better term—wandering spirits. The investigators believed the spirits drift between buildings, based on their energy needs. Another spirit was female, the investigators indicate.

However, they do believe they came in contact with "the man in the suit." This may have been the spirit that other customers and employees have seen in the Nobles. Based on the description, this spirit could possibly be the spirit of the country legend.

Sellers isn't so sure. He doesn't get the sense that Williams is the spirit behind the haunting at the Elite. The researcher says that the restaurant sits in a very spiritually active place of the city—a nexus of paranormal happenings and hauntings. The spirits could be one of several, according to Sellers, and not all fit Williams's description.

However, Sellers has heard of a few other places that those searching out the country legend's ghost in the city where he once lived could look. People—including, reportedly, a bunch of country and western musicians and songwriters like Alan Jackson—say they have found signs of Williams's spirit in a Montgomery cemetery. They claim the singer's grave in Oakwood Cemetery is haunted. On Halloween, you can expect to find a few tours—even some led by an undertaker in a hearse—of this graveyard and Williams's grave is the highlight of the tour.

While the cemetery is full of other ghosts, Williams is the only spirit in Oakwood that has a country song about him. Alan Jackson recorded the tune, "Midnight in Montgomery," a song that describes the singer's visit to the grave of Hank Williams while heading to a New Year's Eve show. (If you remember, Hank died on New Year's Day.) The ghost of Hank Williams appears and thanks the singer for paying tribute.

As our paranormal guide to haunted Montgomery, Sellers said that lots of people do come to the grave of Hank Williams and sing a few of his songs. Some of those folks have been stunned when—after they finish playing—they hear the faint notes of a Williams's song wafting in the southern breezes. They believe that Williams is trying to communicate with them.

Several other paranormal investigators report that they have made contact with a spirit in the cemetery and have gathered evidence through electronic voice phenomena (EVPs). EVPs are recorded files that researchers analyze for messages. Typically the researchers can't hear the voice or noise when they are investigating the site, but emerge out of the static when they examine the file later. According to some ghost hunters, they have recorded voices at the site that some say sound a little like Williams.

Another strange phenomenon that people have experienced in Oakwood is usually just referred to as "the mist"—which might remind you of the mist that appears at the Ryman. People who visit Williams's grave have watched as a white fog appears near the section where a group of Confederate soldiers are buried and moves toward the singing legend's grave.

You can find Williams's spirit in other places in Montgomery, but you might be surprised at one of the spots where witnesses have claimed to see Williams's ghost.

"Of all places, the next one might surprise you," Sellers said. "Hank has also been seen near city hall."

You might not expect Williams's ghost to hang around city hall, but Sellers said that, indeed, several people have claimed to have seen the singer hanging around the landmark. So, why would Williams—who didn't exactly have a cordial relationship with law enforcement and the legal system—haunt a courthouse? Well, a lot of people don't realize that Williams had spina bifida, a crippling and painful disease. Williams was not able to work the fields as most people did where he lived, so he was forced to find another way to make a living. Williams became a street musician, so he knew his way around Montgomery and knew the best places to play. He played the street corners near city hall and perhaps his spirit remembers the generous tips there.

KNOXVILLE, TENNESSEE

The swath of paranormal activity traces Williams's death ride like a trail of crushed beer cans tossed from a blue 1952 Cadillac. Each town he stopped in seems to pick up a little of that lonesome spirit energy.

Williams stayed at the Andrew Johnson Hotel while he was staying overnight in Knoxville during the journey. The hotel has since been converted into government offices, but Williams has refused to check out, according to witnesses. Reports seep out of what was once the tallest building in Knoxville that a ghost still haunts the former hotel's halls and that many people think it is Williams.

Stories filtered out that Williams's spirit was still present in the hotel shortly after his death. People said they frequently saw a figure practically fly down the halls, usually after normal hours. There was never an exact description of just what this figure looked like. From most accounts, it was moving too fast for the witnesses to identify this speedy shadow, so there's no way to tell if the apparition is Hank's, or whether it's not one of the thousands of other souls who stopped by the Andrew Johnson.

But there are a few clues left behind by the ghost that makes people believe that it's definitely the ghost of Hank Williams. A few musical notes, that is. Besides the shadow darting down the halls, guests also heard someone singing—and it sounds a lot like a Hank Williams song. When they checked on the source of the performance, no one was around. The halls were empty.

Most folks wondered if the spirit would stop haunting the hotel once it changed hands. Never one for a nine-to-five routine, Williams seems to have adjusted to the new owners. Rumors suggest that the ghost of the country legend keeps making appearances and keeps singing those classic Williams odes. For most paranormal researchers, it's just a matter of connecting the dots. A tall, thin shadow and those familiar tunes are evidence enough that the spirit behind this activity is none other than Hank Williams.

OAK HILL, WEST VIRGINIA

We'll end our tour of haunted Hank Williams sites, appropriately enough, at the last stop on his legendary tour, as well as the last stop of his mortal journey: Oak Hill, West Virginia.

The small town that was known for little prior to 1953 became the focus of the Hank Williams legend when the singer died en route to a concert. Since then, Williams's fans make the trek to the town to see where the singer died and speculate on the enduring mystery that has surrounded his death. They may not tell you it to your face, but many of these fans are hoping for more than a brush with the past during their visit—they are hoping that they can come face-to-face with the legend himself, or at least his spirit.

Several ghost stories have filtered out of the West Virginia town that the country music superstar has never left. In one incident, a man reported that he was walking by the infamous gas station where his driver discovered Williams had expired and the Old Tyree Funeral Home where Williams's lifeless body was taken soon after. As the man walked, he began to hear music. He couldn't tell what song it was, but, make no mistake about it, the song was one of Hank's. Whoever was singing the song had that distinctive Williams warble and slight yodel. He had the pitch and delivery of a man who has seen trouble, but he keeps his head up. Suddenly, the man sees the outline of a skinny, tall man. The figure becomes clearer. He's wearing a white suit and a cowboy hat. By this time the witness was sure that this wasn't just an early-morning cowboy, this was the ghost of Hank Williams. Puffing on a cigarette, the spirit of Hank looked at the witness and tipped his hat.

Then he vanished.

And that is just the way ole Hank would have planned it.

HANK, THE GUARDIAN HONKY-TONK ANGEL

Now, most people who knew Hank would tell you that he was no angel. Hank himself would have been the first to tell you that he was not a celestial being of any order. But at least one family in Mississippi would have to disagree with all of these parties.

The following story of an angelic encounter of the honky-tonk kind was sent to Mary Lynn Stevenson, a psychic-medium with strong country music connections and a frequent visitor to Nashville, back in the 1990s. She wrote about it in her column about the unexplained.

According to Stevenson, a mother of a high school girl wrote that one autumn evening she handed the keys of her car over to her daughter, Deborah, who was in charge of carpooling a bunch of her friends to and from the homecoming dance. The girls had a great time at the dance. As the evening wrapped up, Deborah collected her friends and taxied them home. One-by-one, the responsible teen dropped her friends off safely at their houses. As she heard the last door close and saw the last porch light flicked off, Deborah knew it was time to drive home. She was a little exhausted after a night of fun and dancing—and chauffeuring.

On moonless, exceptionally dark nights, even the most familiar roads can seem like uncharted territory. It's no surprise what happened next. Deborah was driving on a highway that she rarely drove on before that night and took a wrong turn. As she rode through the dark countryside, the landscape and buildings looked less and less familiar. The needle on her gas gauge dipped ever closer to the big E, and we're not talking about Elvis. The pocket with her money—the only gas money she had—was precariously close to empty, too. Even if she did find a gas station, could she even afford enough fuel to make it home?

Flutters of panic settled when she saw the lights of a store ahead of her. Maybe they had a phone that she could use to call her mother. That panic returned when she discovered that the pay phone was dead.

Deborah drove off to find another store and, as the miles stretched on and the fuel gauge fell even farther, she finally spied another halo of store lights. Unbelievably, the phone at this store was dead, too! Maybe she could at least buy some gas. But the flutters of panic turned into flaps of fear when she discovered that the crumpled dollar bills that she was certain that she had stashed away were nowhere to be found. The panic turned to meltdown, and she broke into sobs. Somehow, between the fingers covering her eyes and the endless tears that rushed down her face, she saw a man exit the store. She'll never forget what he looked like: a big old cowboy hat rested on his head and he was decked out in a brown suit. The suit looked like it had gold threads stitched into the seams. He was tall and lanky with a kind face and voice.

"What's wrong, little lady?" the man asked.

Through heaving sobs, she told him her story.

The man in the brown suit and the ten-gallon hat listened patiently. When she was done, he told Deborah not to worry. He gave her a few dollars for gas and any emergency phone calls she might need to make and offered her directions home. But the tall, kind man had some advice for her: "Go straight home," he warned her emphatically. "Go straight home."

He didn't really have to tell Deborah twice. She was ready for the horrific evening adventure to end.

Deborah watched the man walk away, disappearing into the night. Once Deborah composed herself, she decided she would go into the store and try to find out the man's name. Her good southern upbringing and manners dictated that she should really thank him, she thought. Oddly, not only did the store clerk and fellow customers not know the man's name. They never saw him in the store! That bizarre twist in her tale signaled a strange end to a strange night, but it wasn't completely the end of the tale.

Over the next few days, Deborah avoided telling her mom about getting lost or her run-in with the kind, lonesome stranger, until one day, her mom suddenly asked her, "Did you have any trouble coming home from the dance?"

Deborah admitted she did run into trouble, but that a man had helped her. Deborah's mom then revealed that, on the night of the dance, she had a premonition. In fact, a surge of sadness and concern flooded over her that night. She felt strongly that her daughter was in trouble. She prayed that God would send a guardian angel her way to help. They both agreed the kind stranger in the cowboy hat and brown suit must have been an answer to that prayer.

But the mystery was only beginning. Days later, mom and daughter were flipping through the pages of a country music magazine together. Her mom loved reading stories about their favorite stars and seeing those pictures. As they turned to one page of the magazine, Deborah recognized a familiar face.

"That's the man," she told her mom, as her finger pointed emphatically at the picture. "That's the man who helped me that night after the homecoming dance! I'm sure of it."

Her mom knew exactly who the man in the photograph was. And it could not be the guy who came to the rescue of her daughter. "He's been dead for decades," she assured her daughter.

But Deborah was convinced. She insisted that this was her guardian angel. Her eyes fell on the caption: Hank Williams Sr.

From then on both the mother and the daughter were sure that God sent Hank Williams as a guardian angel to guide her home on that strange night.

NOTES FROM HANK'S SPIRIT

Stevenson, who lived in Nashville and helped out at many country music functions, said this wasn't the only ghostly encounter with Hank Williams that she heard about. In fact, she possibly experienced her own run-ins with the spirit of Hank Williams. As a psychic, she is used to getting impressions, but she never knows—literally—when the spirit might hit her. One time, while walking around the Country Music Hall of Fame and Museum in Nashville during a function, she received a strong impression that Hank Williams wanted to talk. And when Hank wants to say something, he wants to say something.

Stevenson sat down and took out a pad and paper. The words started to flow out of her hand, although she was not conscious of writing the words. It wasn't even in her handwriting; in fact, she never saw handwriting like this before. This is a process that most psychical researchers call "automatic writing." The spirit used the medium's hand to write out a message. When the message was through, Stevenson had a full handwritten page.

Although Stevenson has since forgotten the message of the note, she actually did give the note to Jett Williams, Hank's daughter. Jett immediately recognized her dad's handwriting and has the note to this day, according to Stevenson.

FINAL THOUGHTS

So what can we make out of all these Hank Williams ghost stories? His spirit appears to have no geographic borders, appearing to people across the country; nor does it seem to have any demographic borders—these stories are told by everyone from big country music fans to people who do not have any particular interest in Hanks's music or the man. Some stories are pretty fanciful, but some are based on firsthand encounters that appear legitimate.

Could all of these stories just be merely examples of ghostlore, little folk tales spun by people who want to keep the memory of their favorite country stars around just a little longer?

Perhaps.

But those who believe that Hank Williams Sr. never really left the mortal plane of existence throw one more piece into the supernatural jigsaw puzzle of the singer's life and career. They say Williams left a hint in the title of the final tune that he released shortly before his untimely death, a song that rocketed to the top of the charts, hitting number one at nearly the same time that Hank embarked on his last ride.

The name of that song?

"I'll Never Get Out of This World Alive."

CHAPTER 2

JOHNNY CASH:
THE MAN IN BLACK'S
COLORFUL PARANORMAL LEGACY

No one did more for country music than Johnny Cash. Even though, sometimes, the world of country music appeared to turn its back on him. As he neared the end of his life, he continued to write and perform, but Nashville wasn't buying it—or recording it. They had moved on to younger, softer, and more mainstream acts.

But Cash—as some called him—refused to go down without a musical fight. In the end, an entirely new generation of music fans from an entirely different genre found him and, through him, discovered country music. Recorded by rock producer Rick Rubin, Cash cranked out "American Recordings," an eclectic collection of originals and works by some of the greats such as Leonard Cohen. It was his eighty-first album, and it tore back up the charts and the videos from the album were picked up by video music channels.

The album was a fitting way to close out a historic career. Johnny Cash didn't leave a mark on country music; he burned a swath a mile wide down the corridor of one of America's most cherished art forms. It's no surprise to many fans—and especially ghost hunters—that Cash has refused to relinquish his spot on the earthly plane with the tenacity that he clung to the charts. What is surprising is where he chose to do so. Fans might equate Johnny Cash with the rural south, the hard-working, hard-living south of his childhood and the psychic center of so many of his famous hits. But, according to several witnesses, Cash's ghost is catching the warm rays and enjoying the laid-back vibes in the Caribbean clime.

Cash's home-away-from-home was once part of a plantation that most refer to as Cinnamon Hill in Jamaica. (The island paradise, I should point out, is full of mysterious activity and is considered the most haunted place in the Caribbean.)

The property has what most islanders consider the most beautiful view of Montego Bay, an idyllic stretch of Jamaica's most famous shoreline real estate. But things weren't always so idyllic in Jamaica, nor were things so peaceful in the home where Cash retreated to for a little rest and relaxation. The tension and tragedy that is part of Cinnamon Hill and Jamaica's history makes several ghost-hunting groups who investigate the haunting think that if Johnny Cash's ghost is still haunting the property, he may not be alone.

Several paranormal research teams, including famous television paranormal group members, have investigated Cinnamon Hill and revealed the estate's paranormal—and often painful—past. Slaves worked on the plantation and, often, were punished by confinement in the dank basement of the property. It's better described as a dungeon, according to most of the visitors to the property. Bear traps were hidden on the plantation's borders to keep slaves from running away.

This fear and pain seems to be embedded in the home that Cash called his home-away-from-home. Investigators have picked up evidence of the haunting and lots of Cash's friends and family members that visited his island retreat have reported run-ins with ghosts. Cash also reportedly witnessed some of this paranormal activity and wrote in his autobiography, *Cash: the Autobiography*, that "Cinnamon Hill has its own spirits, presences, and very personal memories."

He carefully delineates between the odd but explainable things that happen in the old house with the odd but unexplainable events that occur there.

"There are ghosts, I think," Cash writes. "Many of the mysteries reported by the guests and visitors to our house, and many that ourselves experienced, can be explained by direct physical evidence—a tree limb brushing against the roof of the room in which Waylon [Jennings] and Jessi [Colter] kept hearing such strange noises, for instance. But there have been incidents that defy conventional wisdom."

One of the events that rests in that "defy conventional wisdom" part of the spectrum happened as Cash was hosting a group of friends and family at his house. He says that a woman appeared in front of six people in the dining room. The woman—who, guests agree, looked like she was in her early thirties and wore a full-length white dress—walked through the kitchen door and toward the double doors on the opposite side of the room. The doors were shut, but that didn't matter to the ghost. She walked right through them.

Seconds later, the shocked group heard crisp knocks. Cash says it sounded like "rat-tat-tat. rat-tat"—on the other side of the door.

Patrick Carr, who helped Cash write his book, had something similar happen. While staying at Cinnamon Hill, he heard that same distinct rap—"rat-tat-tat. rat-tat"—one night, but quickly fell back to sleep. It was just the ghosts, he thought.

Cash, too, felt comfortable with the spirits and, even though the ghostly appearances could be unsettling, never felt threatened by their presence.

"We've never had any trouble with these souls," writes Cash. "They mean us no harm, I believe, and we're certainly not scared of them; they just don't produce that kind of emotion."

Cash says the family's paranormal encounters on the property also included a strange event that happened as he and his wife, June, escorted their young son through the old family cemetery, another haunted feature of the property. Cash said that as they walked through, his four-year-old son, also named John, suddenly piped up that his brother, Jamie, was buried there. June was mystified by the statement, but when she leaned down and searched the well-worn headstone in front of them, sure enough, the grave marked the final resting spot of a man named James. He died there in the 1770s, Cash wrote.

Cash also heard about other ghosts who haunted the Caribbean island, many not to far from his Cinnamon Hill Great House. One of the most infamous was the Annie Palmer story. He even recorded a song about this White Witch of Rose Hall, a woman who reportedly killed her husbands and tortured her slaves in one of the island's most terrifyingly haunted properties, a plantation called Rose Hall. Palmer, the legend goes, was raised in Haiti, the voodoo-infused Caribbean island. When her parents died, her Haitian nanny not only raised her, but taught her voodoo and other forms of witchcraft. She later married a wealthy man and moved to Rose Hall. Suddenly, her husband—and numerous male slaves—began to disappear. Eventually, a slave—or slaves—killed her, but many islanders believe her spirit, a spirit that was too evil even for hell, lives on.

Visitors to what is now one of Jamaica's top paranormal tourist destinations have testified that they witnessed a range of supernatural activity on the property. Some have said that they have seen bloodstains appear on the walls and floors; others have reported hearing footsteps and a baby screaming.

A paranormal team from *Ghost Adventures*, a Travel Channel television series, explored the paranormal side of both Rose Hall and Cinnamon Hill. They used a range of high-tech equipment, including electromagnetic field (EMF) detectors and electronic voice phenomena (EVP) devices, to verify the haunting more scientifically. Another device checks on variations in temperature along with EMF swings, the team said.

The EMF and temperature readings, for instance, spiked whenever the team crossed on the floor above the infamous dungeon where slaves were punished. They asked the guides on the tour if there could be natural reasons, for instance, wiring problems in the floor that were causing the odd readings. The guides said there was nothing below them—except the dungeon.

Unexplainable noises interrupted the investigation on several occasions. When the team checked, they couldn't find any reason for the noises.

By using copper dowsing rods, the team supposedly came in contact with another entity on the property. However, one of the strangest findings during this research trip indicates that Cash has joined the citizens of the Jamaican spirit world. According to the team members, when they reviewed the recordings they noticed an anomaly. Someone at some point during the investigation says, "I do." The team instantly recognized that voice.

It sounded like Johnny Cash.

The singer may be joined again with his wife in the afterlife, too. The team gathered for a flashlight session to contact other spirits on the property. By unscrewing the lens of a flashlight so that the bulb is just barely connected to its battery source, the light will flash on and off when it is exposed to subtle vibrations. Ghost hunters say that a spirit can create vibrations to respond to the questions posed by the researchers using the device. In this investigation, the entity identified itself as June Carter Cash. The impromptu interview may have revealed that June is still deeply connected to her former vacation home, or possibly some of the items she left behind. In fact, there were still pillows in the mansion that were crafted by Cash's wife, as well as some of her favorite pieces of furniture.

The team was convinced that even though Rose Hall and Cinnamon Hill are travel destinations, enjoyed by thousands of tourists, one of country music's most famous couples may be among an elite group of permanent residents.

TELEKINETIC CASH

Most people who have attended a Johnny Cash concert would tell you that the singer had something special, a personal power. Charisma? Star Power? Maybe. But people who knew him personally said he had a spiritual power that was just as warm and just as magnetic as his stage personality.

Cash was steeped in spirituality. Just as he used music to explore life and relationships, Cash delved into religions and belief systems to explore the spiritual realm. As we will discuss, his buddies Johnny Horton and Merle Kilgore were instrumental in the development of the country legend's spiritual—and often paranormal—powers, according to Steve Turner's biography on Cash, *The Man Called CASH*.

Sometimes, those supernatural powers were a little too potent for even Cash to control. In one instance, Cash went to meet with the Kilgores at their home. Cash seemed really taken by the couple's music room. Album covers and gold records adorned the walls of the room and it just had, apparently, a good vibe for Cash.

Cash always felt at peace and centered in the place. He felt so much at home that he asked the Kilgores for a special and perhaps—unless you knew Johnny Cash personally—weird favor from the couple. He asked them if he could have some time alone just to meditate in the room.

They obliged the request. Kilgore's wife brought Cash a cup of coffee and the singer closed his eyes and began to meditate. There's no information about how long Cash was in this meditation, or how he was meditating. All the couple said is that at some point they heard a loud "POP"!

Kilgore and his wife went to the room and looked up to the ceiling. They noticed that a crack had formed in the once pristine ceiling!

The loud noise also roused Cash from what must have been a deep and intense meditation. He, too, looked up, saw the destruction and said, "Oh. I'm sorry. I just ruined your new music room."

"How did you do that?" a stunned Merle Kilgore said.

"Just meditating," Cash replied nonchalantly. "I got the power too strong."

JOHNNY'S PARANORMAL PARTNERSHIP: JOHNNY CASH, MERLE KILGORE, AND JOHNNY HORTON

Johnny Horton was known as one of the best saga singers in country music and rock and roll. It was a category that he kind of created for himself.

Once a rockabilly star, Horton carved his own niche in between country and pop music as the rockabilly craze started to fade. Saga songs, in contrast to the quick, biting beats of rockabilly, featured a big, bold sound combined with epic lyrics, usually drawn from the pages of history. He created sensations with songs, including "The Battle of New Orleans," "North to Alaska," "Sink the Bismark," and "Johnny Reb."

All those songs were big hits for the singer. The last one that was mentioned—"Johnny Reb"—was not only a million-seller, but it was special for Horton for another reason: the song stood as an auditory monument to his collaboration with one of his best friends and a fellow spiritual seeker, Merle Kilgore.

Kilgore was—and is—regarded as one of country music's best songwriters. He cowrote "Ring of Fire" with June Carter Cash for Johnny Cash, which became one of the legend's biggest hits, as a matter of fact. Cash later said that the famous horn section of "Ring of Fire" came as a result of another paranormal power of his: he had the ability to dream hits. He said shortly after hearing a demo of this song, he went to sleep and had a dream that he was singing the tune with a backing of a mariachi band. The distinctive sound of the hit, many country music experts believe, set it apart from other country song arrangements and allowed the tune to transcend from yet another country hit to a musical masterpiece.

Kilgore was no stranger to the occult forces that shaped musicians' careers either. Kilgore's wife claimed that he dreamed a song into existence for his buddy, Johnny Horton.

According to the songwriter's wife, she was sleeping and Kilgore woke her up at about 3 a.m. (I'll point out that many paranormal experts believe that 3 a.m. has unique spiritual properties that allow the spirits—creative and otherwise—to flow through.) She said he was writing a song in his dreams. When she told her husband about the incident, Kilgore had no idea what she was talking about. She went to the reel-to-reel tape recorder, insisting that Kilgore had, perhaps in some type of somnambulistic trance, recorded the tune he had dreamed. The songwriter, however, was still in the dark.

He turned on the reel-to-reel and, just like his wife said, there was the song that would become—with only a few changes—"Johnny Reb," made famous by his bud, Johnny Horton, just a short time later.

According to Cash, Horton paid that favor forward when he used his own supernatural songwriting gift to assist the Man in Black with recovering a mysterious tune. Cash said that he had a dream that fellow country pioneer Webb Pierce was singing one of his songs, but when Cash woke up he couldn't remember the lyrics. He knew that Horton was a hypnotist, so he had his friend put him in a trance to try to recover the lost lyrics. It worked! The song—"I'd Still Be There"—was a hit, too.

Kilgore didn't just tap into the supernatural to help him write songs, sometimes he used the supernatural as subject material. He wrote the song "The Bell Witch" about Tennessee's most famous ghost story. The song references the true story of a family that was assaulted, driven from their home, and maybe even killed by the ghost of a woman who feuded with the patriarch of the family. Kilgore perfectly recounts the main points of the haunting in his lyrics. He also reveals his own understanding of supernatural phenomena. The truth is, Kilgore was an expert on paranormal lore, a trait that fit in nicely with the mystically bent friendship of Cash and Horton.

It was the friendship between Kilgore and Horton that led to one of country music's most wild ghostly whodunits, a tale that may also offer a piece of evidence that proves there is a bridge between the living and the dead. The story, according to Merle's son Stephen and some other sources, goes like this:

Both Horton and Kilgore had a mutual interest in the world of the supernatural, as mentioned. They were particularly intrigued by what happens to the soul when a person's earthly life runs out. They—along with their other spiritual and musical sojourner, Johnny Cash—consulted the same medium named Bernard Ricks. Ricks seemed to have some connections with "the other side." Stephen said that Ricks had intervened a few times in the lives of Kilgore and Horton, as well as other country stars.

Maybe stories of Ricks's predictive prowess were in the back of Horton's mind when he showed up at the Kilgore's porch clutching one of his prized possessions, a custom-made guitar. Horton told Kilgore he was giving it to him. Kilgore, though, tried to stop him. Not that he didn't love the guitar; it was beautiful. But he knew it was the guitar Horton performed on during his shows and must not only be worth a fortune but also should remain a keepsake for his friend.

Still, Horton insisted. He wanted Kilgore to have the guitar.

And then Horton dropped a supernatural bombshell on his songwriting-fishing buddy. He said he was going to die. According to Merle's son, Horton said, "Merle, last night I had a vision that I am going to die, and I am saying goodbye to all of my friends."

The two friends discussed one other morbid topic. They knew the story about Harry Houdini. The late, great magician had given his wife a secret code so that when he died and tried to reach out to her—possibly through a psychic medium—that she would know the message was legitimate. Horton and Kilgore devised their own code, a code that they would share with no one else.

Sadly, the prediction of Horton's death was accurate and his death, like his life, would be tinged with occult weirdness. The story, according to numerous sources, indicates that Horton had a bizarre phobia. He was afraid of intoxicated people and became worried that he would meet his end because of a drunk person. Before a show in Austin, he didn't want to go on stage. He became convinced that if he went near the stage or the bar that a drunk would kill him. Despite Horton's misgivings, the show went on without a hitch. Horton and some of his crew jumped into his Cadillac and headed toward Shreveport. As the car began to cross a bridge near Milano, Texas, when Horton saw, to his horror, that an approaching truck was driving wildly, smashing into one side of the bridge and then the other. The truck smashed into Horton's car, killing him and injuring his passengers.

When the police checked on the driver of the truck, they reported that he was intoxicated. Horton's bizarre fear of drunks was realized and his dire prediction came true.

Kilgore was devastated. For Johnny Cash, the death was even harder to take. He had refused a collect call from Horton just before the crash. It was a decision the singer regretted all his life. But, while Horton wasn't able to reach out to Cash at the end of his life, he did pop in to say hello after his death.

A few versions of the story exist, but, according to Kilgore's son, his dad was visiting a radio station and chatting with his friend, a radio announcer. Bob Lockwood was covering a baseball game and, probably hoping to chew up some time, decided to introduce his songwriting friend to the audience and play his new tune.

Before he started the record, Lockwood announced: "I have with me a great singer-songwriter, Merle Kilgore. Here is a brand-new song that Johnny Cash has just recorded, a song that you and June Carter wrote together. Merle, tell the listeners what's the name of this song?"

Kilgore said that the title, of course, was "Ring of Fire." As the record played and Kilgore and the DJ chatted, a phone call came in from a woman who said she was a psychic who attended a weekly meeting of psychics and people interested in mediumistic phenomena. They had met the night before and received a strange message when the group attempted to contact spirits through a Ouija board. As the hands of the mediums began to glide effortlessly across the board it appeared to rest on several letters. The letters, the mediums noted, appeared to spell out two names.

M-E-R-L-E and K-I-L-G-O-R-E

The problem was, because nobody in the group was a big country fan, the name was basically meaningless. They certainly wouldn't have been able to predict—by normal means, at least—that Merle Kilgore would have appeared on the radio the next day. Remember, Merle's appearance was pretty much an accident.

It wasn't just Merle's name that crossed the spiritual transom. The psychics claimed a message—and a weird one at that—came through. Letter-by-letter, the psychics pulled the following sentence from the Ouija board: "The drummer is a rummer and he can't hold the beat."

Kilgore was flabbergasted.

This somewhat strange and meaningless message for the psychics was the very code that Horton and Kilgore agreed on to prove that one or the other had successfully crossed over.

Horton apparently did.

CHAPTER 3

ROY ACUFF:
THE KING OF COUNTRY MUSIC WON'T ABDICATE HIS MUSICAL THRONE

Although Roy Acuff may not have been blessed with—or cursed by—as colorful of a country music career as his contemporary, Hank Williams, Acuff's contributions to country music are just as pioneering and his legacy just as long-lasting as Williams's. They do, after all, call Acuff "the King of Country Music" for a reason. Acuff takes on Williams in another category: country music spooky ghost stories.

While Williams's ghost, just like his Luke the Drifter persona, has been spotted all along the highways and byways, reports of run-ins with Acuff's ghost are primarily centered in a house he built near his beloved Grand Ole Opry Theater.

Early in his career, Acuff considered the chance to sing on the Grand Ole Opry radio show a life-changer and he never forgot the opportunity. He loved performing on the radio show so much that he built a home in what became Opryland plaza, just to be close to the action. The performer was active at the Grand Ole Opry nearly until he died in 1992—and he may still be active there after his death.

Acuff was born in 1903 in Maynardville, Tennessee. His father, who was a lawyer, a minister, and a fine fiddle player, introduced him to music and the musical influences of the church, which played an important role in the musical upbringing of lots of the country stars we examine in this book. He performed as a singer and front man for a number of bands for years, but his big break came singing on the Grand Ole Opry in 1938. Listeners enjoyed his performance on the show that night so much that he was asked to be a regular on the weekly show. The rest is musical history; the haunted history of the Roy Acuff House, on the other hand, began more than a half century after that pivotal Grand Ole Opry show.

Since Opryland is so haunted—something we'll cover in an upcoming section—you might assume that the Roy Acuff House, just like other buildings in the area, could be haunted by any number of wandering souls. But paranormal researchers tie it directly to Acuff's passing. They are quick to point out that people began to report paranormal hauntings at the building in 1992, shortly after Acuff passed away.

The incidents became so numerous and occurred so regularly that word got out about the house soon after Acuff's passing. Once the house was turned into a museum, more people—staff and visitors—began to observe the strange phenomena. The building's haunted reputation zoomed to the top of Nashville's paranormal top ten. One of the first things that witnesses noticed were the odd footsteps. They said they heard someone walking through the house. Those were definite footfalls that would echo down the halls, these witnesses suggested, not the creaks of the house settling. But when these witnesses chased down the sound—perhaps expecting an intruder or a lost guest—they found no one. The building was empty.

When people began to notice an inexplicable light show, the rumors that Acuff was still haunting the building began to escalate. Lights would turn on and then turn off, all by themselves. You might think this is easily debunked: it's just a case of loose or faulty wiring, right? But it turns out the management of the museum had electricians check the wiring and everything seemed to be fine. There's something else about the activity that makes electrical issues a less likely source of the problem. The lights aren't flickering. They turn on for a long time—and then turn off. It's like someone is controlling the lights, witnesses say. In an upcoming story, we'll discover there are other places that the ghost of Acuff apparently likes to fiddle with the lighting.

Acuff lets the staff know he's around in other ways—strange ways. The staff blames the singer for a few pranks. Over the years, several employees reported that items disappeared and then reappeared a few hours or a few days later, sometimes in a totally different spot than where they remember placing them. Several stories have circulated of staff members tossing something on a table or a desk and then, when they go back to retrieve the item, find that it's gone. Disappeared. Vanished. Then, just when they forget about the incident, they'll walk into a room and there—in plain sight—will be the missing item.

Skeptics would easily discount the missing-objects phenomena. It's just a bunch of forgetful employees blaming the paranormal on their own incompetence. But that theory starts to shake in light of other evidence. Some folks have claimed not to be the victims of a missing object paranormal prank, but to have actually seen these things move without any human—at least a living human—nearby. The witnesses watched—horrified—as items start to slide down desks and table tops or across mantels. Chairs have moved by themselves, too.

For those familiar with the haunting, this odd phenomena is just Acuff still going about his business—a business that he always loved—in a place that he called home for most of his life.

MORE ACUFF HAUNTINGS

We could easily discount the stories of Acuff's eternal attachment to his Nashville home, if it weren't for other stories about the King of Country Music's ghost popping up in other haunted hot spots in the music city.

Nashville is full of ghosts and some say that Acuff is one of the leading paranormal attractions at one of Nashville's most visited landmarks. According to those who worked at the Opry House, the site where some of country's biggest names have performed and continue to perform, Acuff kept watch over the stable of talent that hits the stage at the Opry. He must still want to share the stage with them, too.

Most of the accounts came from employees who had the unenviable task of closing up the Opry House once the show is over. The performers are gone. The audience members have snapped their last pictures and have moved on, too. Most of the technical crew—the guys and gals who take care of the light and the sound—have left. It's just a few members of the skeleton crew and the dark, empty, and reportedly haunted auditorium.

In the darkness, employees report a lot of false paranormal alarms. The acoustics are so good that sounds are magnified. Sounds from naturally occurring phenomena sound creepy and supernatural. You can forgive the staff for being a little on edge. However, the employees say they adjust to the weird sound effects—and that makes their reported run-ins with the paranormal even more compelling and believable.

One activity that the employees have no rational explanation for is the light and curtains show. Several staff members say they go through their closing checklist, making sure the lights are off and the curtain closed. However, as they make their way out the door, the employees can hear the lights switching on and the curtains move. They go back inside and—low and behold—the stage lights are on and the curtain is pulled back like another act is hitting the stage.

The most likely spirit suspect is Acuff, these workers say. They believe the King of Country Music just wants to feel the floor of the stage beneath him and imagine the roar of the crowds just one more time.

It should be noted that a serious flood in 2010 harmed Roy Acuff's former home, as well as several other buildings in the area. The theme park has also been closed, although there is talk about rebuilding. As of the writing of this section, Acuff's home is still standing. We don't know whether or not it's still paranormally active.

CHAPTER 4

PATSY CLINE:
HAUNTING VOICE, HAUNTED LIFE

No single vocalist—male or female—ever captured the often contrasting subtleties of country music quite the way Patsy Cline did. She sang with all the vulnerability and sensitivity of an angel and all the toughness and single-mindedness of a long-haul truck driver roaring through the endless American highways at night.

That was Patsy: tough and vulnerable, sensitive and focused.

Born in Virginia, she seemed to have absorbed that vulnerable toughness, or tough vulnerability, from an environment full of dichotomies. Patsy's family was poor and her father abandoned them. But her mother made sure Patsy and her siblings had lots of love and, generally, provided a happy childhood for the children.

Say what you want about Patsy Cline, but she was resilient.

Her life followed that pattern, a roller coaster of ups and downs, of tragedies and triumphs. Just as her career took off, she was in a car crash. A second one, in 1961, nearly killed her. She was thrown through the windshield and her recuperation took weeks. But she trooped on, heading out on the road six weeks later, scarred and on crutches. By late 1961, her version of a Willie Nelson-penned tune, "Crazy," was a cross-over hit and her career hit superstar status. She was the first female country performer to headline her own tour and typically received the same billing as male stars.

Around 1962 or 1963, Cline began to tell friends that her roller-coaster ride of a life was pulling into the station. She didn't have health problems. She didn't feel threatened. It was, she told them, just a sense that she had. Cline began to give away personal items and she wrote out her will, with a twist of irony, on a Delta Airlines stationary. At least one friend remembered her saying that she survived two near-fatal accidents, the third one would either be a charm or it would kill her. That sense of foreboding turned into reality during what was supposed to be a quick airplane trip back to Nashville. In March 1963, Cline was a passenger of a small plane that crashed during a spell of high winds and inclement weather.

She was buried in Shenandoah Memorial Park, a cemetery in her hometown of Winchester, Virginia. There is a single sentence emblazoned on a bronze grave marker that is almost as much a prophecy as it is a memorial: "Death Cannot Kill What Never Dies: Love."

In addition to the numerous tributes to Cline's contributions to country music—the books, movies, and plays about her life—a clock tower above her grave reminds us of how her voice and life resonates with us even today. The clock daily tolls at 6 p.m.—the hour of her death. But, as we'll see, there are other ways that Cline reminds us that her spirit hasn't exactly left the stage.

People still claim to run into the ghost of Patsy Cline. Most of these stories come from the spots connected to her life—and to her legend. Cline was one of the few women of country music at that time who wasn't afraid to mix it up with the boys and meet them on their own turf. She hung out at bars and could be heard joking with the guys using her particular term of endearment, "Hoss." Even today, there are reports that she's still hanging around in those bars. Patrons of some of country music's most legendary bars, like Tootsie's Orchid Lounge, have said they see a woman who looks a lot like Patsy Cline appear on a stool at the edge of the bar—and then vanishes—or she'll stroll into a crowd of couples on the dance floor and just disappear.

Other haunted incidents have happened at Nashville landmarks that we will discuss in detail, like the Ryman. It's usually fans that spot her or spot a perfect Cline lookalike, who disappears before the fans get close enough to identify her either as the spirit of Patsy Cline or a really good impersonator.

DREAM HOME'S RESTLESS SPIRIT

Since Cline's childhood was so turbulent and tenuous, it was natural that she wanted one thing once she was discovered and the checks began to flow in from performances and record sales: her Nashville dream house.

Comparing Cline's dream house—a 4,000 square foot ranch-style home—to the mega-monstrous mansions of today's country and western stars, might make Patsy's dream seem a little underwhelming. In fact, in its day—the early 1960s—the home was quite the showplace and worth serious money. It had some cool features, too—like an intercom system that would keep pumping music to the music-loving owner no matter where in the house she roamed. Tragically, she only lived a few months in her dream house before she was killed. Maybe that's why, some paranormal theorists suggest, she keeps visiting.

After Cline died, the home became somewhat of a curiosity piece. Patsy's husband, Charlie, sold the house. The home has exchanged hands at least three more times. During that time, Patsy's dream house was included on tourist maps, something that the new owners probably weren't happy about. They didn't like fans showing up on the doorstep expecting tours of their favorite singer's homestead, either.

Eventually, the home was sold in 2011 to a real Cline fan, Steven Shirey, and he didn't mind the visitors so much, according to Shirey's hometown paper, the *York Daily Record*. But he said another guest made him think that he wasn't just a fan of Cline's, but he was also her housemate. According to the owner, a series of inexplicable encounters convinced him that not only was the home haunted, but it was haunted by his favorite country star.

Patsy was known for walking at midnight. The ghost in Patsy's old house is known for walking at midnight—and all hours of the night—in this house, he said. Shirey, who still owned the house at the writing of the article in 2014, told reporters that he could hear what sounded like high-heeled shoes walking across the floor in the upstairs of the home. Trying to find an explanation, Shirey initially blamed his two Chihuahuas. The clickety-clack of claws might mimic the sound of high heels, but he later realized that his dogs weren't to blame.

During restoration efforts, Shirey asked his sisters to come to Nashville and help him. They accepted. The sisters went to work stripping the wallpaper. As they worked, their brother noticed that the upstairs gas fireplace was lit. In fact, the fireplace lit by itself a few times. Shirey blamed his sisters, but they said they had nothing to do with it. It was already mid-summer in Nashville and, as anyone who has ever stripped wallpaper will tell you, the last thing you would want while completing this hard, sweaty job is a little extra heat circulating through the home.

His sisters began to suspect the house was haunted, a suggestion Shirey laughed off, at first. But more strange things began to happen. Another odd manifestation, for example, occurred in the house from time to time that led the owner to suspect something paranormal was going on. The lights in the mostly unused back bedroom turned on by themselves. Obviously, someone was using it—but that someone wasn't necessarily a living resident in the home.

Eventually, Shirey joined his sisters in their assessment that the house was haunted, although he joined them reluctantly. He took one more step to verify his now growing suspicion that Patsy was haunting his home—he reached out to Cline's daughter. She told Shirey that she thought the house was always haunted. Maybe her mom just joined the party. She was known to do that.

Shirey told the reporter that his skepticism is on the edge, "I never really believed in spirits or any of that stuff, but there has to be something to it. Something is causing these things to happen."

Some paranormal experts have another theory. They point out that Shirey tried to restore the home to its early '60s splendor and that may have set the haunting to a more up-tempo setting, according to some paranormal experts. Experts say that restoration efforts are often known to unlock spiritual energy. And Patsy might have just found the new interior design just too familiar and too cozy to leave.

Shirey's story does receive corroboration from at least one other former owner of the home. Singer Wilma Burgess claimed that she experienced strange activity, not unlike the events that Shirey experienced, that convinced her that she was sharing the home with Patsy.

MORE PATSY HAUNTINGS

There's one more ghost story that involves Patsy Cline, but in all likelihood, it's probably not Patsy's ghost who haunts the quaint The Inn on the River. There's no record that she stayed at the inn, which is located in the historic community of Zoar, Ohio, or even visited the town. But it could be that Patsy's sweet vocals have reached across the divide between the living and the dead to connect yet another Patsy Cline fan on the other side of those once-thought impenetrable walls.

According to several reports, the sounds of Patsy Cline music fills the halls of the inn, but when people try to find the source of the music, they come up empty.

The hauntings connection with Patsy is unclear. The inn seems to have lots of other supernatural activity and, in fact, the whole town of Zoar seems to be more paranormally active than most towns. Most experts on the haunting trace the ghost back to an account of a man—known only as George—who drowned near the inn. Maybe George just has good taste in music?

As we'll discover in upcoming chapters, Patsy haunts lots of places that have an extensive paranormal reputation, just like the Inn on the River. The Municipal Stadium in Shreveport, site of the famous country music radio show the *Louisiana Hayride*, and Memorial Stadium in Kansas City, boast of encounters with the late legend of country music.

Back in her hometown of Winchester, the paranormal Patsy run-ins are increasing. People have collected photographic evidence at the site. These visitors have snapped pictures at her home and at her grave, and when they analyze the photos more closely, they see strange images and orbs. Most take these odd anomalies to be signs that Patsy is still around and reaching out to make contact with her fans.

As we'll see in the next chapter, Cline's close friend Loretta Lynn has had her share of paranormal encounters, but she has never reported an encounter with the ghost of her friend. Lynn, however, felt her mentor's presence while staying in the Cline residence shortly after the singer's tragic death. Lynn wrote the song, "Haunted House," about that experience.

It may be that the song, which may not have been written about an encounter with a ghost per se, does seem to be prophetic.

CHAPTER 5

LORETTA LYNN:
THE COAL MINER'S DAUGHTER'S RICH SUPERNATURAL VEIN

People who live in eastern Kentucky believe that the hills and hollows that are carved into the spine of the Appalachian Mountains of eastern Kentucky are alive with spirits and lost souls that they call *haints*. Country music legend Loretta Lynn, also known as the Coal Miner's Daughter, is one of those believers.

Lynn's encounters with haints began as a young girl in Butcher Hollow—a small town in Johnson County, Kentucky—and continues, according to recent media reports, to this day. The run-ins with the strange and unknown have ranged from the deeply troubling to the benignly spooky.

She writes about the first time she saw a ghost—or a haint—in her autobiography, *Loretta Lynn: Coal Miner's Daughter*, and it happened, conveniently enough, on Halloween. According to Lynn, she was engaged in the trick part of trick-or-treating with a friend one Halloween night. They were rubbing soap on the windows of the home of a local lady. Lynn looked into the window and saw the woman who owned the home—the intended victim of the trick—working in the kitchen. Then Lynn turned around and saw the exact same woman walking in the garden. Her friend saw the haint, too. They both broke into a full sprint and ran away from the house. They never went back.

When Lynn bought a plantation in Hurricane Mills, Tennessee, she found not just one haint, but dozens. Unlike the trick-or-treating adventure back in Butcher Hollow, however, she couldn't run away from these haints.

In fact, the country music legend suggests that these haints led her to this über-spooky property. Lynn said that she and her husband were driving on back roads outside of Nashville when they got lost. During the road trip, they saw a for sale sign in front of a huge house. The Lynns just happened to be looking for a bigger home. Their fortunes were growing—and so was the family. The plantation home was a perfect fit.

When Lynn bought the property, she initially thought it was just a plantation home. It turns out, the sale included the whole dang town. It also turned out that many of the residents of the town that they just bought weren't all living citizens. A whole village of paranormal natives called the property, called Hurricane Mills, home. The first sign that the property was paranormally active happened almost as soon as Lynn—now a famous country star—her husband, and their large family moved in. She noticed that the door that connected her room with an adjoining room used as a bedroom for her young twin daughters would open and close by itself. Of course, it could be just a faulty hinge or an unbalanced floor. But as a person who knew a thing or two about the supernatural, the phenomena immediately tweaked Lynn's paranormal paranoia.

More strange things began to happen that confirmed Lynn's suspicion. The twins, who were very young at the time, began to tell their mother tales that they talked to people in their bedroom. The guests wore funny clothes and sported odd hairstyles, they said. The hairstyles may have been odd for the twentieth century, but the way the twins described the styles, the look would have fit with how people wore their hair in the eighteenth and nineteenth centuries, Lynn reasoned—hairstyles that her young daughters would never have seen before.

As Lynn learned about her new home, she discovered new—and sometimes unsettling—information about the property, information that gave the country singer and her family solid reasons why Hurricane Mills was paranormally active. For instance, the family noticed an odd feature of the home—a dark, dank hole with an iron-barred gate in the roof. They learned that it was a slave pit, a place where the plantation owners jailed slaves who misbehaved. Once, while Lynn and a friend were watching television, both heard the sound of someone walking across the porch. The sounds of the footsteps were so pronounced and obvious that Lynn turned on the porch light and looked out. No one was there. Lynn and her friend returned to watch television, but their viewing was interrupted once again by an even more disturbing sound. This time, not only did they hear the sound of footsteps walking across the porch, but they heard what sounded like a chain being dragged across the wooden planks of the porch. Lynn and her friend guessed that the sounds were coming directly above the slave pit.

More ghostly visitations followed and each one seemed to reveal another facet of the property's past. The family found out, for example, that a Civil War skirmish happened on the grounds of the plantation—and that some soldiers who perished during the battle were buried on the property. The soldiers have a funny way of reminding the family that they're still on guard. Lynn said that her son was fast asleep when something roused him. He looked toward the foot of his bed and there—standing in full military dress—was a Confederate soldier.

The family also saw the spirit of a woman dressed in white and who seems to be weeping. The ghost was seen pacing up and down the balcony. They soon referred to the sad spectre as "the moaning woman."

Over the years, Lynn experienced the paranormal activity in the home in other ways. The family heard footfalls echoing down the hall and up the steps, even when the rest of the family was nowhere near the area. Decorating was a hassle in the new place, too. Pictures and paintings had the odd habit of hanging perfectly straight on the wall one minute and then, on the next glance, the artwork would be crooked. The family found no rational explanation.

The singer said she felt electric shocks at times and places in the home that were impossible to predict. It wasn't like static electric shocks from rubbing her feet across the carpet. This sensation felt like someone—or some presence—was passing through her.

Supernatural activity may creep you and me out, but not the Coal Miner's Daughter. What would typically scare most people intrigued Lynn. Each incident, in fact, pushed Lynn to try to understand why the haunting was happening. She decided to contact the spirit—or spirits—that were haunting the property.

Lynn decided to reach out to the spirit world through a series of séances at her house. The reaction of the spirits even surprised supernatural-savvy Lynn.

During one séance, the table where Lynn and her friends were sitting began to move on its own after, they believe, the group came in contact with a spirit named Anderson. The group pressed the ghost to reveal more information about himself, but the spirit grew agitated. The table began to vibrate, and then it began to shake violently. Finally, the table lifted completely off the ground and flipped over!

The would-be paranormal investigators believe that Anderson may refer to the original owner of the home, James Anderson. He was buried on the land, too, some say. The name also matches Buela Anderson. Buela, legend has it, was a young mother whose baby died. She slipped into a deep depression and died. Could this be the same melancholy spirit—the moaning woman—that Lynn saw on the balcony?

Lynn has invited paranormal investigators and psychics to confirm her own encounters at Hurricane Mills. For paranormal researchers, investigating the property is a treat, not just because they get a chance to meet a country legend, but because teams rarely come up empty during an investigation there. The evidence collected is impressive. Words like "dig" and "ground"—and other references to burial—were heard during sessions when teams attempted to collect EVPs. The mentions may be references to the Confederate soldiers buried on the land. Another interesting EVP was the word "moan" that was collected by a team. The researchers believed this referred to the moaning woman. One of the most important pieces of taped evidence for Lynn was the sound of a spirit calling her name.

In this section, we've looked at people who haunt: the ghostly trail of Hank Williams and the spirit-filled high jinks of Roy Acuff. Lynn seems to be an anomaly. She's not a person who haunts; she's a person who gets haunted—and that may have a lot to do with her own psychic gifts.

In fact, Lynn's paranormal adventures in Hurricane Mills are a small part of her supernatural legacy. She not only had ghostly experiences, but the singer is known as a psychic herself. Shortly after Lynn married, she and her husband moved across the country and away from her family in Butcher Hollow. She didn't have a phone, but she could always sense when her neighbor, who was one of the few residents of the rural area to have a phone, would show up with a message that someone was trying to reach her. She could also predict when letters would arrive from her mother.

She's also had premonitions that mostly came in the form of dreams. Lynn had a vivid dream of seeing her father in a coffin. A short time later, her father died from a massive stroke. Lynn had felt guilty for leaving her family back in Kentucky. She especially felt guilty about not seeing her father before he passed away. But it turned out she had a second chance. Lynn went back to her old home in Butcher Hollow, years after her father died. When she walked toward the house she saw the ghost of her father relaxing on the front porch.

A COAL MINER'S HAUNTER?

Loretta Lynn grew up in the shadows of the richest vein of coal that was ever mined in the United States. Johnson County's Van Lear earned a famous—or notorious, depending on whom you ask—reputation as a sprawling stretch of some of the country's biggest, deepest, and most productive mines. Lynn referred to the Van Lear in her song "Coal Miner's Daughter" and in the title and title song of her album, *Van Lear Rose*.

Though most of the deep mines have been shuttered over time, especially during the mid-twentieth century, the shadows of the once booming Van Lear mining operations still spread over the region, paranormal theorists say—except they say that a lot of those shadows are ghosts. Those supernatural shadows that now stalk the Van Lear mines and communities are probably related to the history of the region, a history that was filled with tales of misfortune, violence, and treachery. As any ghost hunter will tell you, when there are tragedies, there are deaths and when there are lives taken violently, or taken too early, you have unsettled spirits. Several of the worst coal mining accidents happened in Van Lear operations. Violence between workers, and violence between workers and management were part of the fabric of daily existence in Van Lear and surrounding towns and villages.

You don't need to convince the volunteers who staff and guests who visited the Van Lear Coal Miners' Museum. The museum is based in the same building that used to serve as the headquarters for Consolidated Coal Company, one of the major coal companies in the area. During the first half of the twentieth century, this building was the center of Van Lear's mining operations. But the building was more than that. According to local historians, it was the community's nerve center. In good times and in bad times, in boom times and in busts, this was the site where people gathered to talk about or plan on how to deal with the situations. Now it's the hub of the town's haunted activity.

Museum volunteers say that the ghosts manifest themselves in strange ways—from the sounds of footsteps to feelings of unseen presences. One of the weirdest phenomenon in the museum is the feeling that children are in the building—and are trying to interact with visitors. A museum worker said she felt a hand grasp her arm. Others have felt this firm hold during their visits. Several witnesses had testified that they have sensed children crawling in their laps.

This relates to some of the other supernatural occurrences. The sounds of children laughing waft through the halls, long after the place is closed to visitors. There are simply no kids in the building, say the volunteers who hear the laughter.

It's not just that kids appear as ghosts; ghosts seem to appear to kids. In one heart-stopping moment a young girl—probably around two years old—wandered off from the tour. The adults looked for the girl all over the museum. When they finally saw her in the library, they immediately stopped. She was talking to someone. Her eyes were fixed on someone. But who could it be? There was no one in the room to their knowledge. They walked closer and heard the little girl jabbering away, but when the adults followed the stare of the child to her conversational partner, they realized there was no one there. The library was empty—at least to their non-spiritually tuned vision.

Eventually, the accounts of paranormal activity became so widespread that the museum administrators called in the experts. Paranormal research groups that investigated the hauntings for the staff are mostly convinced that the place is haunted and several members of those groups are convinced it's *really* haunted. They have collected evidence, including the picture of—at least what looks like—a man's face. Another ghost hunter said a female voice clearly said, "Be careful," as the investigator began to climb a ladder. The kicker is that there were only two people in the museum—both of them male.

Researchers also complained about a hidden fee in investigating ghosts there—they said they always needed to buy extra batteries for investigations. The ghosts, they say, drain the energy from the batteries for their flashlights, cameras, and other electronic devices they bring for their research. This anecdotal evidence of the Van Lear haunting backs up accounts from other paranormal theorists who suggest that ghosts and spirits use energy from these batteries to manifest.

In case you're wondering, the museum seems to be paranormal researching friendly. They are willing to deal with groups who want to investigate the building, but they do charge a nominal fee.

CHAPTER 6

ELVIS PRESLEY:
HOUND-DOGGED BY HAUNTINGS

Elvis Presley is the King of Rock and Roll, but that was after the history books had pretty much been written. Prior to his ascension to rock's highest throne, he actually considered himself more of a country and western singer. The King went by a much less dignified title: the Hillbilly Cat.

A pioneer in blending musical styles, the Hillbilly Cat skirted the edges of country music and was never fully embraced by the establishment until much later in his career. He eventually shared one other thing with country legends, like Hank Williams and Roy Acuff, though: ghost stories.

Since Elvis's passing in 1978, ghost stories have swirled around the places that the King graced with his presence during his life, including his home dubbed Graceland, Nashville recording studios where he laid down a golden path of hit records, and, oddly, at the Ryman Theater, after all it was one of the places where Elvis's raw and somewhat raunchy brand of music was rejected.

We'll discuss Elvis's haunting at the Ryman a little later when we review the haunted history of this hallowed site of country music.

THE GRAVES OF GRACELAND

If you were looking for Elvis from the late 1950s to the late 1970s, you would travel to Graceland, the King's homey mansion in Memphis. If you're looking for the spirit of Elvis, you would still travel to Graceland.

Graceland, which was originally owned by a newspaper publisher, S. E. Toof, is one of the most haunted spots in the city. Toof, by the way, gave Graceland its serene name after his daughter, Grace, who eventually inherited the property.

Elvis snagged the property off the Memphis real estate market in 1957. His fans had finally overwhelmed his family's modest home and forced him to seek a place with a little more property, privacy, and security. Of course, this white-columned, neoclassical mansion was the site of the last breaths of the King of Rock and Roll, who died in the mansion in 1978.

You might think that the stories that spirits haunted Graceland began to appear after Elvis's death. You would only be partially correct. Graceland's reputation as a haunted locale began way before that. Big personalities—just as big as Elvis's ample personality, some say—inhabited the mansion and may have left their psychic mark on the property. There are four graves at Graceland: Vernon and Gladys Presley, Elvis's parents; Minnie Mae Presley, Elvis's grandmother; and Elvis's own resting place. There's also a memorial for Elvis's stillborn twin brother, Jesse Garon.

Where you find big personalities—and especially where you find graves—you'll probably find ghosts. Everyone knows that.

Family members with huge spirits, like Elvis's mother, Gladys, and his grandmother, Minnie Mae, whom he nicknamed Dodger, are said to haunt the property with the King. There's a good chance that Elvis heard stories about encounters with the spirits of his family members and perhaps even told his friends and hangers-on about his own brushes with the spirit world.

Some people claim to have seen the apparition of Gladys on the property. These reports do not necessarily come from the omnipresent Elvis fanatics who surround Graceland on a daily basis, but from reliable witnesses, such as friends and family. Staff members, too, have seen the figure of an older woman. While the image is often described as fleeting and transparent, most people quickly match the image with pictures of Elvis's beloved mom.

Years before these sightings, though, the spirit of Gladys was making her presence known to her beloved family members. Minnie Mae said she heard strange noises in the mansion's attic. She described them as rustling noises—like someone was rummaging through the boxes and mementos that the family stored in the attic. She believed it was Gladys's ghost. The stories spread through the family, eventually reaching Elvis's new bride, Priscilla.

Priscilla was all alone in the home—which seemed bigger and emptier when Elvis was gone—and a rain storm moved in. Maybe she, like hundreds of victims of horror movies, was just one of those people who when they are alone in a giant, spooky mansion during a thunderstorm decide to go to the attic in search of ghosts. Whatever the reason, Elvis's wife decided to explore the attic. She made her way up the steps and tried to find a light to illuminate the pitch black room. When she finally found the switch and clicked on the lights, Priscilla saw racks and racks of dresses and clothes once owned by Gladys.

Intrigued, Priscilla stepped closer. Like the lightning crackling around the home, an electric sensation sizzled through her body. She sensed the joy of her departed mother-in-law.

Priscilla began to try on Gladys's clothes. She put on some of the hats, too. As she did, Priscilla felt what could only be described as a hug. She felt like Gladys—the mother-in-law she never really knew—was reaching from the beyond to give her a hug. Elvis's wife wasn't scared; in fact, she said it was a special moment that she'll never forget. She bonded with Gladys again that night.

It wasn't just family members and staff who have had an unexpected encounter with the supernatural at Graceland. Since Elvis shared so much of his life with his fans, there's no reason to doubt that he wouldn't share a hunk of his afterlife with them, too.

There is one encounter that still provokes debate among the Elvis Presley loyalists. Soon after Elvis died and his home was open to visitors, one man said he strayed from the tour and saw someone in the pool house—someone who looked familiar, but, if news reports were correct, shouldn't be there. The witness said he saw Elvis in the pool house talking to people. He quickly snapped a picture. The photo made the rounds and the fans quickly divided into three camps: There was the "It was a fake" camp; there was "It was the ghost of Elvis" camp; and there was the "Elvis is still alive" camp.

In fact, right after Elvis died, people began to see him—or his twin, or his ghost—all over the country. He was seen scarfing down a Big Mac at McDonald's. He was working as a gas station attendant. A whole genre of truck driving ghost stories centered on stories about truckers who pick up Elvis, sometimes he's heading to Graceland, other times he's trying to escape Memphis.

After a lot of those accounts were labeled urban legends, some fans began to believe that Elvis may be dead, but he wasn't exactly gone. A story circulated that at least one tour of Graceland went from a fun afternoon remembering Elvis to a supernatural brush with the departed King of Rock and Roll.

It goes like this: A father, mother, and daughter were moving along with a group of fans touring the mansion. They had just entered the trophy room, a gymnasium-sized room that contains a lot of the awards that were given to the singer, along with costumes and other Presley paraphernalia. It's a tour highlight for most fans.

The mother, who could have sworn her daughter was right at her side, checked around the crowd making its way through the trophy room to find her daughter. She wasn't around. It was strange because the daughter was sticking pretty close to the mother's side throughout most of the tour. The panic level began to increase as the mother wandered through the aisles looking for her daughter but was unable to spot her. Panic turned to pandemonium. Security put the property under lockdown and each member of the tour began to look for the girl.

With a huge collective sigh of relief, the girl was found unharmed near the tiny graveyard that Elvis referred to as Meditation Garden. The sighs of relief turned to sighs of exclamation when the once-lost girl told her parents and the other members of the tour group about the tour of Graceland she received from a special guide.

She said that a nice man in a white suit took her by the hand and gave her a quick tour of the mansion and then, when he was done, dropped her off by the grave. He then, in her own words, "disappeared." There was no one on the tour who was wearing a white suit, nor did security officials see anyone who fit the descriptions. Some people immediately began to suspect that this wasn't a mortal guide, but an angelic helper—and a few even suggested it was Elvis. These people say that details of the description fit Elvis perfectly. He was fond of white clothes, he loved kids, and he loved Graceland.

Other witnesses have had peripheral encounters with Elvis's ghost—and maybe even the ghost of Elvis's horse. One woman said that while visiting Graceland, she noticed a magnificent black horse. No sooner did she see it then it reared up and bolted toward the barn, almost as if someone was calling it. But the woman neither saw nor heard its handler.

Intrigued, the witness sought out a guide and asked if Elvis's horses could still be at the barn. He replied that, no, the horses that Elvis kept, or their lineage, are being groomed at another site and no horses were at the barn that day.

The woman, however, was convinced that she saw the horse.

ELVIS'S OTHER HAUNTS

As we'll see in upcoming stories, the ghost of the Hillbilly Cat is prowling other places in Memphis and Nashville, but Elvis's spirit isn't just relegated to places in Tennessee. Elvis's career took him all around the country, and his spirit apparently became attached to certain cities that matched his larger-than-life appetite for adventure, cities such as Las Vegas and New Orleans.

Believe it or not, Elvis suffered his first career dip when his rockabilly juggernaut rolled into Sin City. Right after he had steamrolled through the South and then conquered television, Elvis's management thought he would blow away the crowds in Las Vegas. The audiences who watched him were polite, but, let's face it, he was no Frank Sinatra. Viva Las Vegas would have to wait.

Over the years, Las Vegas and the musical tastes of its casino goers began to change. They started to embrace Elvis. Heck, they didn't embrace him, they gave the King and his white jumpsuit a big old bear hug. To say thank you, Elvis left a little hunk of his burning love—and his smoldering spirit—in the city.

It's no wonder the King haunts the Heartbreak Hotel in Las Vegas. It's almost his namesake. Named after an iconic Elvis tune, the hotel continues to be the site of some of the most vivid paranormal encounters with the singer. Long after Elvis left Las Vegas permanently, guests, workers, and performers at the hotel have claimed to see him. And hear him.

The Wedding Chapel—scene to countless Elvis-themed weddings—is one place you'll want to visit if you're looking and listening for Elvis's spirit. Witnesses say they've heard Elvis songs when no one was around—and the sound system was turned off.

We all know how photogenic Elvis was. That hasn't stopped in the afterlife either. Some patrons to the Heartbreak Hotel claim there are photographic anomalies in the pictures they took at the hotel. The phenomena range from simple orbs—often discounted by skeptics—to ghostly shadows that resemble the King, which are a little harder to explain away.

If you can't make reservations at the Heartbreak Hotel, Elvis's legacy and haunted legacy still shines on at the Las Vegas Hilton. The hotel was the site of some of the legend's most famous Las

Vegas concerts. He stayed in the thirtieth floor of the Hilton—and he hasn't checked out yet.

People—especially people who work backstage at the Hilton—have said they saw the spirit of Elvis. The workers say it's the flashy Elvis that's haunting the Hilton. They claim to have seen a man in a white jumpsuit appear out of nowhere and walk around backstage. The spirit disappears as quickly as he appears. The ghost has also been seen near the stage elevators.

BIG E IN THE BIG EASY

As Elvis toured the South during those heady early days of his career, he found a certain affinity for the people and the party-filled atmosphere of New Orleans, Louisiana. He loved performing in the city, but he loved hanging out there, too. One of his first movies, *Kid Creole*, was sort of a homage to the King's love of the city.

When Elvis died, the people of New Orleans were among the most shocked. They weren't shocked, however, when his ghost started to show up in some of his—wait for it—haunts.

When Elvis was alive, he stayed in the city's famous French Quarter, known for its historic balconies that are the perfect perch for slinging beads during Mardi Gras festivities. Some of those revelers have claimed to see Elvis on the balcony. Before you start to doubt the sobriety of these eyewitnesses' accounts, some of these people have gathered photographic evidence. In some cases, the ghost of the King appears as a full-bodied apparition, to the point that witnesses think it's an Elvis impersonator. Other times, his image must be traced in a thin film, or fog, and still other times, he shows up in photographic anomalies, like weird flashes of light or orbs.

Elvis's ghost in New Orleans is not stuck in one era. Though most people have seen the Hillbilly Cat version of Elvis haunting the streets of New Orleans, there have also been reports of movie star Elvis ghosts, Las Vegas Elvis ghosts, and even chubby Elvis ghosts.

This all just goes to show that in the afterlife, just as in real life, Elvis always wanted to give the fans what they wanted.

CHAPTER 7

MINDY MCCREADY:
OF ANGELS, DEMONS, GHOSTS, AND CURSES

Country music has never shied away from tragedy. And tragedy has returned the favor by never shying away from the lives of country musicians. The thread between magic and tragic is razor thin for country musicians. No one in the modern country music era seems to embody this twisted embrace between musician and misfortune, as well as the connection between inspiration and spirits, quite like Mindy McCready.

Her life and career began with as much promise as any country music superstar, but, under the blazing spotlights of fame and fortune, she burned out and imploded just as quickly—a superstar turned supernova. All along her path, though, hints of the paranormal followed along.

McCready started her country music career in her teens, graduating early from high school to pursue her dream. By eighteen years old, she had a contract and watched as her album, titled, prophetically enough, *Ten Thousand Angels*, sold more than two million copies. The album's ascent up the charts was powered by the strength of hit singles that struck a chord with country's more independent, empowered female audience, "Guys Do It All the Time" and "A Girl's Gotta Do (What a Girl's Gotta Do)."

In a few years, though, she would need to tap every single one of those ten thousand angels. After a few monster albums and sold-out concerts, the sales and the hit singles began to dry up. Rumors of her substance abuse and relationship troubles, on the other hand, began to increase, as did tales of her involvement with the spirit world. Her world seemingly spiraling out of control, McCready finally went public with her paranormal experiences on the television show *Celebrity Ghost Stories*. She spoke specifically of an event in a Scottish hotel that changed how she felt about the supernatural forever.

The singer described the hotel she stayed in during her 1999 tour as old and beautiful with a majestic staircase. The hotel, like lots of other old, beautiful Scottish buildings, was reportedly haunted. McCready felt this mysterious force when she entered the building, but she later sensed this force was trying to communicate with her—or at least reach out to her.

One thing she noticed was the windows. After a smash performance at a nearby concert hall, she was hoping to nestle into her hotel suite when she realized that the rather large windows were open. Probably not so supernatural for windows to be open, she thought, but it was curious. The evening was cold and rainy—it was Scotland after all—and it's unlikely that anyone opened the windows on purpose. She shrugged it off, hopped up on the sofa to access the windows, and with some struggle, closed the windows before going about her nightly routine.

A little bit later, while preparing for bed, McCready heard the sound of rainfall, so she returned to the room and received a shock—the windows were open again.

Now the country star became worried. The windows were too large and heavy to open by themselves. She wondered whether she was alone. Did someone—maybe a staff member—enter the room and open the windows? A quick check around revealed no one was with her in the room—or, so she thought. Events would forever convince her that someone was with her that night, and that someone wanted to help her.

The phenomena increased during the night. The hotel room grew increasingly colder, becoming much colder than the warm and comfy space she arrived to find.

When McCready went to cover up to avoid the ever-decreasing temperatures, she accidentally kicked an empty duffel bag, one that she was sure she had left in the downstairs portion of the hotel suite.

"And then I started thinking, 'well how did the bag get unpacked in the first place,'" she told the crew of *Celebrity Ghost Stories*. "I left it downstairs and who brought it up here? Did the hotel unpack my bag for me and put it at the foot of my bed? And why was the duffel bag the one that was unpacked and brought up here?"

Deep inside, McCready knew the answer to these questions. The singer knew that this string of events—that the hotel staff would select a bag, bring it to her room, and then unpack the items—was unlikely.

She checked the seemingly empty bag. But it wasn't totally empty. Inside there was a journal or a notebook. It wasn't her journal. Respecting the privacy, McCready went to put the journal back in the bag and left it in the downstairs section of the hotel suite.

That's when she heard footsteps—firm, distinctive hard-soled shoes—walking across the room. McCready scanned the dark hotel room for this mysterious walker, but she saw nothing but shadows.

"I was paralyzed with fear," McCready said.

She screamed out for the presence to identify himself or herself—or itself. The footsteps immediately stopped.

The now-terrified superstar turned her attention to the notebook. She got it and opened it up. When she did, the gently burning fire in the fireplace suddenly erupted.

"It was like breath coming from the fire," the singer explained.

McCready felt that the fire, the footsteps, and the windows that opened by themselves were no mere coincidences. The phenomena were evidence that some spirit or force was pressing her to look at the notebook. She opened it and discovered it was her boyfriend's diary. She said that in the book, her soon-to-be-ex-boyfriend detailed his affairs with other women. As she threw the book into the fire and watched the offending pages burn, the fire "breathed" again, just as it did a few moments before. Sounds like a great country song, doesn't it.

But there's a supernatural twist.

McCready went downstairs to talk to the staff. She asked one man if the hotel was haunted.

"And he said, 'yes, ma'am, it is' and that I should have nothing to worry about because it was haunted by nuns," she said.

Before it was a hotel, the building served as a nunnery. The nuns were still buried under the structure; the staff member informed McCready and added, "If they visited you, it must mean that you needed a mother tonight."

She said that sometimes powers from beyond are needed to teach those on an earthly plane the right lessons. The incident at the hotel changed how McCready faced the supernatural.

"Sometimes we need help from somewhere else, from beyond. I'm not afraid of the supernatural anymore," she said.

But the supernatural would come calling to McCready again.

Despite this paranormal intervention, McCready struggled to get her life and career back on track. Each subsequent album was less and less successful, until the requests for concerts and the contracts for new albums dried up. Her personal life plummeted to new lows. About the only times that McCready could garner any headlines is when news of an arrest, suicide attempts, and substance abuse binges hit the entertainment news and blogs.

Then, in 2013, her life swung completely out of control. Her boyfriend, David Wilson, committed suicide. That was bad enough, but McCready was wounded even more deeply over allegations and rumors that she killed her boyfriend. She denied the accusations publicly, but the damage had been done.

As her world fell apart, McCready told a friend that she experienced one bright spot. The ghost of her departed boyfriend had visited her. She said he came to her room. The singer also reminisced about one of the last movies that the couple watched together—*What Dreams May Come*. It turns out, the film was prophetic. The movie deals with a man's search in the afterlife for his wife, who committed suicide.

According to a friend, the movie sparked a conversation between McCready and Wilson. She told the friend, "And I said to him, 'David, if I killed myself … if I ended my life and it was over, would you come find me? Would you find me? Would you go through hell to find me?' He said he would go through anything to find me."

We don't know whether he did. But we do know that on February 17, 2013, McCready sat on the porch of her home, the same place where the body of her boyfriend had been found, and took her own life.

Her fans—who still remember the vibrant but tortured artist—hope she can finally rest in peace.

CHAPTER 8

J. BERNARD RICKS:
COUNTRY MUSIC'S
MAJOR MEDIUM

One of the names that appears in the paranormal history of country music never—to my knowledge or research—strummed a guitar, plucked the banjo, or sang on the Grand Ole Opry's stage. In fact, from most accounts, he was just a simple man—a simple man who just so happen to commune with spirits.

While this man was more of a country mystic than a country musician, his influence as a spiritual guide and medium appears to have touched many of country's biggest names and wielded substantial power that may have changed musical history. The man, Bernard Ricks, or J. Bernard Ricks, is a bit of a mystery—a shadow that has been cast on some of country and pop's brightest stars, including, as we mentioned earlier, Johnny Horton, Johnny Cash, and Merle Kilgore.

There are scant details about how these country musicians became acquainted with Ricks, but the group soon established a relationship that bordered on guru and disciples. Based on some accounts, Ricks was just a postal worker in the Shreveport, Louisiana, area. He attended the Louisiana Hayride shows and became friendly with Horton. The musicians on the show recognized that Ricks had a strange ability to raise the level of their creativity. It was a spiritual power that they could feel. Stories of the prophet's spiritual gifts and the tales of his interventions began to circulate. It turned out that spiking performances with a little extra creative juice was just the start of the spiritual guide's power. He could save lives, too.

According to one story, Ricks—out of the blue—called Merle Kilgore's wife and told her to check on the couple's daughter. She was taken aback, knowing that the little girl was okay because she just set her down for a nap moments before. But the medium insisted and mom, dutifully yet doubtfully, went to her child's bedroom. She entered the room and gasped. Her daughter was suffocating. The baby somehow wedged her head under the mattress and was turning blue. The medium's call came just in time!

Other friends and family of Horton said that Ricks had known that the saga-singing rockabilly idol was headed for a fatal accident. In fact, as we discussed earlier, Horton himself seemed to have an idea that his time on earth was short, a sense that may have come from his consultations with country music's most important medium. In fact, there are some hints that Ricks warned Horton about his dire future some time before his death so the singer could get things in order.

After Horton's death, however, the messages kept coming through, and Ricks was still the chief operator of the psychic messaging system for the departed rockabilly and country star.

One story that circulated shortly after Horton's untimely demise is that Johnny Cash became convinced that Ricks received a message from the beyond that could only have come from Horton because—much like the message shared between Horton and Kilgore that we discussed earlier—only Cash, Kilgore, and possibly a disembodied Horton could have known the details of this message.

According to an article in the December 1961 issue of *The Chimes*, it all started on the morning of Horton's funeral. Cash and Kilgore, both obviously distraught at their friend's death, were walking alone in Horton's backyard. If you remember, Cash may have been feeling even darker than usual because he failed to answer a last call from Horton. The dark clouds that consumed the sky must have seemed like an exact reflection of the country stars' spirits. Then, suddenly, Cash stopped and said: "You know, Merle, I have a feeling that a miracle will take place today—it is so dark! It will come at a time when the grief is at its height! It will come—and then all these clouds will clear away, and *everything will be as bright as the day!*"

The funeral was a grueling, deeply emotional affair for Cash, who couldn't help but watch Ricks sitting near him. The medium wore a glassy expression on his face during the ceremony, occasionally scribbling in a notebook in a calm, almost trancelike, manner.

After the funeral, the sad procession of friends and family journeyed to the plot at Hillcrest Memorial Park that would be the final resting place of Cash's musical and spiritual brother. The funeral party then went back to the Horton home.

Cash was waiting for Ricks—impatiently pacing, by some accounts—in the front yard. He excitedly asked Ricks for his notebook, which the medium used to jot down his impressions and messages from the other world. In this case, Ricks was writing notes during Horton's service. Although, as Cash must have known, it wasn't Ricks degrading the funeral service by jotting down notes, rather the spirits of the dead were using Ricks as a medium to write messages.

When he opened it, the singer saw some strange symbols—a duck, a guitar, and a fish. (Cash may have recognized the fish as a symbol for Horton's nickname, the Singing Fisherman.) As he scanned through the notebook, Cash saw that some of the symbols eventually became words—crudely written, for sure, but still Cash made out the words.

To Cash's astonishment, the words read: "Bright is this day."

The singer cried out, "It was Johnny! It was Johnny! That's the same thing I said this morning. Word for word!"

Cash was convinced the words referred to the impression he received and relayed to Kilgore earlier in the day: "And then all these clouds will clear away, and everything will be as bright as the day!" Only Kilgore and he were there during this conversation—and neither had talked to Ricks at length before the service.

The article continued, "Johnny Horton had made it back—through his friend and advisor, Bernard Ricks. Both men, loyal friends of Johnny Horton, wiped the tears from their eyes and looked into the starry night. 'It's just as he said, Johnny: It's bright as day up there where he is.'"

While there's no evidence of a falling out between the singers and their spiritual muse, this spiritual circle appears to have been broken. Cash and Kilgore continued their successful careers in the country music industry. Ricks continued to investigate the supernatural. He also wrote about it, serving as a correspondent for *The Chimes* (a leading spiritualist journal at the time), *Fate Magazine*, and other periodicals dedicated to spirituality. Ricks even traveled to the Philippines in 1964 to determine the legitimacy of psychic surgery. As Ricks explains in the piece, psychic surgeons in the Philippines claimed they could remove spiritual obstructions from patients and that these objects were the real cause of cancers, diseases, and other maladies.

The trail on the life of country music's most influential spiritual advisor grows cold at this point. This enigmatic country music medium, like all good spiritual soldiers and just like the spirits that he claimed to contact, seemed to fade away.

SECTION 2

HAUNTED COUNTRY PLACES

Music and the act of worship are nearly inseparable. Name one religious service that does not integrate music somehow in its service—from the soaring transcendence of Bach fugues to the hypnotic drum beat of traditional African religions. Country music is no different. In fact, because of country music's close association with hymns and folk music, it might rely on the spiritual theme than other types of music. And, as you may have guessed, where the sacred and spiritual tread, spirits and ghosts are not far behind.

In the previous section, we discussed country music stars who experienced the supernatural. In some cases, these stars allegedly even became part of the spirit world. In this section, we will find out that it isn't just the people of country music being haunted. The very places where country music is played, heard, and enjoyed are haunted, too. It is, after all, no coincidence that places connected with country music—like the Ryman Auditorium, dubbed the Mother Church of Country Music—are spoken of in spiritual terms.

Country music concert halls and venues are some of the most haunted places in the country. There are also stories of spectres and apparitions lurking in country bars and honky-tonks. Most country paranormal spots are haunted by friendly spirits, but there are other tales of paranormal encounters in country music that are much darker, even demonic. We will review the dark side of country music in this section, as well.

Most would probably argue that live shows are the best ways to experience country music—it is, after all, the closest a person can connect with his or her favorite star. However, the studios where musicians crafted their soon-to-be smash hits rarely escape from brushes with the supernatural.

On the first stop of our tour, we will travel to the capital city of country music and, perhaps not coincidentally, the capital city of many of country music's spookiest ghost stories.

CHAPTER 9

HAUNTED CONCERT VENUES AND MUSIC HALLS

THE RYMAN AUDITORIUM: THE GRANDDADDY OF ALL HAUNTED HALLS

"You're going to Nashville."

For country singers and musicians those four simple words signaled that their dreams of stardom were coming true. Their hard work had paid off and their talent was finally being recognized.

Placed at a nexus of musical and spiritual influences, Nashville is a city of contrasts. It's a big city full of small town sensibilities. It's a hip cultural mecca and a folksy watering hole. Its streets are where wishes come true and its boulevards are where broken dreams finally rest.

Nashville is a city of lights—neon lights and stage lights, spot lights and street lights. The city also has a dark side, some say a paranormal side. Supernatural experts say that war, disease, natural disasters, and economic calamity have filled the buildings and streets of Nashville with ghosts who aren't too happy about the location of their new neighborhood, located somewhere between life and death.

The site of our first stop on this tour of haunted Nashville is a perfect example of this supernatural mixed bag. The Ryman Auditorium has some friendly ghosts, some celebrity ghosts, and at least one dark spirit.

Nestled in the historic center of country music, the Ryman Auditorium is surely the spiritual center of that music. The somewhat austere-looking brick building located on the city's Fifth Avenue is called the Mother Church of Country Music for a reason. Indeed, the Ryman was completed in 1892 as the Union Gospel Tabernacle. That was before it became a place where both secular performers and fans of secular music, alike, were dying to get into. Now, for some of them—dying can't seem to get them to leave.

Though the *Grand Ole Opry* radio show was eventually moved to more modern and more technologically impressive digs in Nashville, the Ryman was the original home of the show that became synonymous with country music. Artists came from all over the country to perform for both the live and the radio audiences and those fans swarmed the Ryman from all over the country to hear performances from country legends—stars like Patsy Cline, Loretta Lynn, and Johnny Cash.

As we have already discussed, the ghost of Hank Williams supposedly haunts the theater. But Williams is not the only suspect in the long list of legendary spirits—or spirit legends—who make their after-death appearances at the auditorium. The Ryman has a haunted history that goes way, way back to an era even before country music filled its acoustically perfect concert hall.

Many experts say that to truly understand why the Ryman is so supernaturally charged we have to go the whole way back to the man who built it: Captain Thomas Ryman. Ryman was a riverboat captain, the owner of a bunch of saloons, and not what anyone at the time would call a good Christian gentleman. In fact, he was not happy at all to hear that the Reverend Sam Jones was in town.

The preacher's sermons were lighting up Nashville and his tent revivals were reforming Nashville's wayward citizens and the captain's best customers. You see, the pastor was casting down verbal fire and brimstone on the citizens of Nashville for gambling and drinking—two of Captain Ryman's major profit centers. So, the captain decided he would go to one of Rev. Jones's revivals to listen to the pastor in person—maybe to heckle him, maybe to confront him. But something happened, something that would change Nashville history forever. The salty, sin-enabling captain didn't break up the revival or ridicule the pastor. The captain converted.

After Ryman's conversion, he built the Union Gospel Tabernacle—which was renamed the Ryman Auditorium after the captain's death—so that the faithful in Nashville would never have to use tents for a revival. Ryman invested $100,000—which was a huge sum of money at that time—in building this revival meeting house. When Rev. Jones preached his first sermon there, he said it was worth every penny, saying, "I believe for every dollar spent in this Tabernacle, there'll be $10 less spent in the future on court trials. This tabernacle is the best investment the city of Nashville ever made."

Captain Ryman still keeps close watch on his spiritual investment apparently. Because he built the auditorium for spiritual reasons, those familiar with the Ryman haunting say that the captain was not exactly thrilled when the auditorium became a performance hall for popular secular acts, too. He made his displeasure known in a big way. Once, when a particularly saucy act (for the time), had a chance to perform at the auditorium, audience members began to hear a ruckus. Sounds—like violent poundings—erupted, causing some fans to think that someone was ripping the theater apart. The noise grew so loud that it drowned out the act that the captain's spirit had taken such a profound dislike to. That's one way to clear the stage.

The reformed captain may be the noisiest spirit in the auditorium, but he by no means is the only spirit haunting the property. Guests, performers, and workers dub another spirit "the Gray Man."

Compared to the ghost of Captain Ryman, this spirit is as subdued as the hue of his nickname. First, he dresses a bit drab. People who have run into the Gray Man say he is dressed entirely—you guessed it—in gray and they say there's even something somber about his demeanor. Another odd thing about this ghost is that he doesn't attend any of the lively performances; he's more likely to show up for rehearsals.

Lots of artists who performed at the Ryman tell stories about scanning the empty seats of the auditorium as they rehearse their upcoming sets and, as their eyes pass by rows and rows of empty seats, they unexpectedly see a man sitting alone. For those who have never heard of the Gray Man legend, they probably assume he is part of the Ryman staff. But other artists, savvy to the legend, know who he is.

Some of the more courageous (or crazy) souls investigate the sighting as soon as they are done with practice. Each time, it's the same story: the witnesses dash off the stage and run toward the seat where they swear they saw the Gray Man, but when they arrive, the man is gone—vanished.

The Gray Man graces more than just the stars of the famous Ryman stage. He likes to appear to the common folk, too. Maintenance workers who clean and fix the auditorium long after the shows are over say they have seen a man—dressed in gray—often sitting in the balcony seats. Just like all the other stories, the Gray Man skedaddles before the workers can approach him.

Who is the Gray Man? All the friends of the Ryman Auditorium continue to debate that question. Although the debaters have not reached a firm conclusion, they have established a few possible theories. One theory is that the Gray Man is just a fan who died and returned to the place he loved the most—the Ryman. Others believe that since the auditorium was built in a town that was devastated by the Civil War, the spirit may be the ghost of a long-departed Confederate soldier. After all, the Ryman was host to several conventions of Confederate veterans of the Civil War. Maybe one of those feisty rebels decided to stick around long after his brothers-in-arms had moved on.

Star Ghosts

Like the eternal evening sky, the Ryman has seen stars come and go, although a few may have extended their stay, one might say, perpetually. We've already discussed the ghost of Hank Williams. He's earned top billing on the marquee of ghostly acts at the auditorium. More than a few witnesses have spotted a foggy apparition that looks a lot like Williams on the Ryman stage.

Patsy Cline, one of country music's first ladies, was a popular act on the Grand Ole Opry, and fans have seen her ghost at the auditorium. Ghost hunters guess that she was so attached to the Ryman in her life that the bond never broke. Like Williams, her apparition is supposed to be blurry, but any fan who has a run-in with Cline's ghost say they can recognize her iconic shape and her brilliant smile.

Then there's the ghost of Elvis. The King of Rock and Roll didn't exactly bring down the house at the Ryman when he tried out for the Grand Ole Opry. In fact, if the legend is correct, Ryman talent scouts basically told the King—and his swivelin' hips—to swivel on back to Memphis and ask for his truck-driving job back. He would not play at the Ryman. (Captain Ryman's ghost must have supported that decision.)

However, years later, none other than Elvis's daughter Lisa Marie may have encountered her father's spirit at the Ryman and is as ornery as ever. The story goes that Lisa Marie, who had her own musical career, finished up a performance at the Ryman and went to her dressing room with her entourage. When she tried to open the door to the dressing room, though, the door was stuck. Not locked. It was stuck. Lisa noticed when she pulled the door back, the door would give a little and then snap back. It was like someone was on the other side, tugging at the door. She pulled harder. No luck. Then she asked one of the burlier members of her group to give it a pull. He pulled it with all of his might—and it did not budge. Another bodyguard jumped in and gave it a tug. Again, no luck.

Eerily, the door would sometimes open—just a crack—and then slam shut!

Exasperated, Lisa Marie voiced her concern and told the paranormal practical joker on the other side that she would call the security guards. At that moment, the group swore they heard a laugh, one that sounded exactly like Elvis's laugh. Then, the door opened easily.

The group became convinced that even though the old guard didn't want Elvis to play at the Ryman during his life, that wouldn't stop the King from playing around after he shuffled off the mortal coil. Lisa Marie probably saw the paranormal practical joke as just another way her dad was still reaching out to his beloved daughter.

OPRYLAND: NEW FACILITIES, "OLE" SPIRITS

In 1974, the *Grand Ole Opry* radio show and concerts, so synonymous with the heydays of country music, moved from the Ryman Auditorium, where the performances (and a lot of ghosts) were hosted for about half a century, to the recently constructed theme park, Opryland. You can't sugar coat this. It was a sad moment for country music history. But it was a hopeful one, too.

Fans were hopeful that the new venue and park would make country more accessible to the many millions—and growing—fan base. Some of the staff were hopeful that a more modern and spacious hall would attract even more fans.

People who believe in the paranormal were split into two camps, too. The staff of the Grand Ole Opry might look forward to a new space where a possible bone-chilling supernatural encounter didn't lurk around every corner and behind every closed door. People who were interested in the paranormal, on the other hand, were hopeful that the fine tradition of country music ghosts would follow, too.

We already know who came out on top in the ghosts-versus-no-ghosts request. We heard, for instance, about Roy Acuff's haunted house at the park. But Acuff's ghost is just one of the dozens of other chilling paranormal accounts that have circulated about Opryland, and especially the Opryland Hotel. These stories indicate that just because you move country music performances, doesn't mean its famous ghosts won't move with them.

Even before the first ghosts started to arrive, word has it that one of country music's most famous ghosts was looking the place over. Late one night, a construction worker was accidentally locked in. Instead of waiting on his rescuers to arrive, the worker began to explore the work site. He swore he saw and heard Hank Williams and another singer practicing one of Williams's songs. Who the other singer was is up for speculation.

While Williams and Acuff are the most famous names among the spirits that haunt the property, another less-known name is probably the most feared. Staff and guests at the hotel have seen the eerie apparition of a woman walking slowly down the halls. They refer to her as Mrs. McGavock. But she has a much more ominous-sounding name, too: the Lady in Black of Opryland.

She earned that moniker because she is often seen draped in a black veil. That's one reason people are sure it's a ghost and not a case of mistaking a living human for an apparition. After all, how often do you see people wearing veils these days? The rest of her ensemble is not of this era, either. Witnesses say her sense of fashion definitely reminds them of the Civil War, or pre-Civil War–era garb.

One staff member writes that he had a run-in with the ghost in 1990. He said he was a retail manager of a store in the hotel that had the unenviable distinction of being open the latest at night. The store closed at midnight, but the manager routinely stayed much later than that, often stocking shelves and completing paperwork until 2 a.m.

Late one night, the manager said he was passing by the staircase that takes guests from the first to second floor and saw the image of a woman in a full gown. Weirdly, he remarked that the image was blurry, not sharp and clear, so he knew it was definitely not a flesh-and-blood person walking down the steps. He also knew he was the only one in that section of the hotel at the time.

Keeping his wits—and Southern charm—about him, he just said, "Good evening, ma'am" and stayed in place. He said the spirit eventually faded away and he went about his nightly duties.

Another group of workers had a run-in, or possibly a glide-in, with the Opryland Hotel's resident spirit, according to Christopher Coleman's *Ghosts and Haunts of Tennessee*. The workers were waxing the floors of the hotel. They looked up and saw the Lady in Black gliding above the spot they just had cleaned. Another cleaning woman saw the ghost and immediately quit, according to the book.

The Lady in Black was also seen in the outlet stores that surround the hotel. After a century-and-change of haunting, she probably has quite the shopping list. Maybe she could finally change out of that black veil.

So who is this mysterious veiled lady? Many people call her Mrs. McGavock, which connects the haunting to one of Nashville's famous historic families, according to most experts on Opryland's paranormal activity.

They say the McGavock family owned the property and its majestic plantation house called Two Rivers House a long time ago. Now a historic destination of its own, staff members who act as tour guides and who maintain the property say that the mansion is the center of paranormal activity. They say they have seen objects disappear right in front of their eyes and heard the sound of footsteps crossing empty halls.

Even though Mrs. McGavock is the prime suspect, experts say she is just one of many spirits—including numerous ghosts of Native Americans and Civil War soldiers—who inhabit the extremely haunted fields and winding rivers that make this section of Tennessee the state's most haunted hunting grounds.

THE MUSIC CITY CENTER: BRANSON, MISSOURI

As we'll discuss, Branson, Missouri, is like a little Nashville—a budding entertainment capital poised to take on Nashville as the capital city of country music. Branson's ghosts are in on the competition, as well. One of Branson's hot spots—and an even hotter haunted hot spot—is the Music City Center, a popular entertainment complex. The building houses a theater and modern recording studios, and is reportedly outfitted with a few spirits, too, including the ghost of a little girl who likes to greet visitors and members of the staff, according to *The Ghosts of Branson* by Charles Kennedy. Workers like to call her Amy. They say she usually announces her presence with a few pranks. Objects will disappear and then reappear, or items will suddenly move. But Amy isn't afraid of going full apparitional.

In one instance, employees who worked the late-night shift heard strange noises echoing from the theater section of the complex. They went to investigate. As they peered into the darkness, the staff members said they could plainly see and hear a little girl. She was humming and tinkering with the equipment. When the workers called out to her, she froze and looked back at them. Then, right in front of the unbelieving eyes of the workers, she vanished.

The sightings tend to freak out new workers, but the run-ins with Amy have become so commonplace that once workers get used to Amy, the fear starts to diminish. In fact, most people sort of like that she's hanging around.

Employees, however, wouldn't mind if another guest ghost would check out. The ghost of an old man haunts the hotel, too, a couple of reports indicate. He doesn't want to play, either, or, at least, he doesn't have quite the same sense of playfulness as Amy. The spirit of the old man—who doesn't even get a nickname—is blamed for a lot of the weird and often annoying activity around the building. Workers point the finger at him any time the power fails, equipment breaks down, or the elevator stops working.

The odd elevator malfunctions can happen anytime—night or day. It seems to happen in all types of weather conditions, so the employees don't blame the problems with the elevator on a passing thunderstorm, for instance. Right before the elevator experiences problems, people also have noticed the elevator lights flashing on, like an unseen finger is pressing the buttons.

Most of the time, the culprit goes unseen, but some witnesses have reported signs of a presence and at least one story suggests workers made physical contact with the ghost of the elevator prankster. According to the story, a group of employees was called to repair the elevator during one of its shutdowns and said they saw an old man exit the elevator room. They called out to him, but he never responded and, as they watched, he disappeared—just like the little girl who plays in the theater of the Music City Center. When the crew entered the room and checked on the equipment, they discovered that a switch has been physically turned to the off position.

There is only one thing that tops the number of rumors of haunted encounters at the Music City Center and that's the reasons for why the ghosts are there in the first place. Actually, nobody knows how the ghosts made their way to the entertainment complex, but it could be that—as we'll find out—Branson is so overwhelmed with haunted activity, these spirits just needed a place to stay in the city.

APOLLO CIVIC THEATRE: FRIGHT AT THE APOLLO

During the Apollo Civic Theatre's long history, an equally long line of country music's biggest names have performed there, from the classic country stars—Little Jimmy Dickens, Merle Haggard, and Tex Ritter—to some of the more modern stars, such as Garth Brooks. The stars and their fans keep coming back to Martinsburg, West Virginia. According to guests and staff, it's not just the stars that come back to the Apollo. The spirits keep coming back, too.

The hauntings in the restored building on Martin Street stretch way back, but one member of the theater group that performs there told a *Herald-Mail* reporter that his first run-in with the unexplained happened in 1975. The theater group member, Mike Noll, told the reporter he was alone in the theater one night when he saw something moving across the back balcony. From his vantage point, it looked as though a bunch of inky shadows were running along the balcony. He also heard the creak of steps, like someone was walking up and down the stairs.

Just another naive ghost hunter jumping to conclusions? Maybe not. At the time of the incident, Noll was a skeptic—"was" being the operative term. He could have easily dismissed what he experienced as the theater settling or some other unusual but natural phenomenon. But this incident was only one in a string of strange encounters people have experienced in the building. He said that his 1975 encounter jibed well with so many other stories that he has heard over the years, as well as testimony from his fellow theater friends, that he became convinced there was something strange—if not paranormal—about the theater.

"You don't know if your mind is playing tricks on you or if it's something serious," Noll told the paper. "I probably wouldn't have believed it if so many other people hadn't seen or heard the same kinds of things here."

What Noll saw and heard that evening was just another notch in a long list of unexplainable events that have caused people—many of whom were once skeptics, like Noll—to change their tune about the supernatural.

It's not just shadows and shapes. Visitors and staff, alike, have endured the full range of paranormal phenomena in the theater, including the manifestation of full-body apparitions. There's a man wearing bib overalls and a brown-checked shirt who haunts the Apollo. Another spirit you might encounter is a woman with a long white dress. Other unlucky witnesses have seen the violent side of the paranormal: they report seeing a man and a woman who appear to be trying to strangle each other.

Not all of the ghostly activity can be seen or heard. Some of it is smelled. The unmistakable scent of cigar smoke wafts through the halls and rooms of this grand theater, even when no one is smoking stogies. One guest became so agitated she broke out in hives when she smelled the cigar smoke while standing in an empty room. Some of the Apollo regulars say that the stogie smell is from a ghost named Charlie. They say the cigar-chomping manager was at the helm of the theater back in the heydays during the 1920s.

Another witness said she had an encounter with Charlie outside of the theater. The woman, who lived in a nearby apartment, could see the theater from her window. She was looking out one evening and saw a man in a fedora lighting up a cigar. He was hunched over and his jacket was pulled up to his ears, so it was hard to make out facial details, she said, but she could definitely see that cigar. The woman figured it was just an actor from the theater. But when the cigar-smoking man also immediately vanished before her very eyes, she knew this was no ordinary thespian. It was such a jarring event that the woman—who knew nothing about the theater's haunted legacy—sought out a ghost hunter. The hunter told her she probably saw Charlie, who must have wanted to stretch his legs a bit after decades of haunting the Apollo.

For some reason, Charlie is most likely to make an appearance during the autumn. That's when most of the reports of cigar smoke smell begin to filter in, or perhaps non-filter in. Nobody knows why Charlie seems to like the fall so much, but it does coincide nicely with the traditional spooky season of Halloween, experts on the case point out.

Charlie is just one of the ghosts hanging around in the Apollo, which shouldn't be a surprise. The theater is situated in a haunted town that's part of a haunted region. The Civil War and an influenza outbreak in 1918 are just some of the tragedies that may have fueled this excessive supernatural activity.

There are so many ghosts that the Apollo has become a training ground for ghost hunters and paranormal investigators. At least one group of ghost hunters, who said they investigated about five thousand cases during their existence as an organization, was called in to check out the premises after receiving a report that someone in the theater was shoved by an unseen force while standing alone backstage. The leader of the West Virginia–based group said that this report, though, was only one of dozens of calls, emails, and conversations that she has had about the haunted Apollo.

SHREVEPORT MUNICIPAL AUDITORIUM: A HAYRIDE INTO THE PARANORMAL

The Art Deco building that stands proudly on Elvis Presley Boulevard in Shreveport, Louisiana, holds a lot of history. Elvis Presley performed at the Shreveport Municipal Auditorium as part of his culture-changing performances on the Louisiana Hayride, a popular country radio show that was broadcast from the auditorium.

Hank Williams and Johnny Cash played there, too, as part of the Hayride.

Once you go inside, you realize that the building—affectionately nicknamed the Muni—isn't just full of history; it's full of ghosts, according to fans, employees, and the occasional paranormal researcher who have encountered supernatural presences at the arena. Elvis, Hank, and Johnny, along with Patsy Cline and an unnamed custodian, have all been added to the extensive lineup of spirits who may be haunting the building. The reports of para-normal manifestations in the Muni include apparitions and audi-tory phenomena—including electronic voice phenomena and odd knocks and groans—as well as poltergeist activity.

The spirit of a custodian is one of the spectral suspects. Many witnesses believe they have seen the apparition of the janitor ru-mored to have died in the Muni, according to some stories. The custodian, however, has some celebrity company. A member of the Convention and Tourist Bureau said that while in the build-ing one evening she saw a figure appear momentarily. She's con-vinced that it was Hank Williams.

The Man in Black is also supposed to haunt the building. A frequent guest on the Louisiana Hayride radio show and per-former at the Muni back in the day, Cash's performances are listed among the auditorium's most memorable. And Cash's ap-pearances don't show any signs of stopping. Witnesses have re-ported hearing Cash's distinctive deep voice in the auditorium, and several people investigating the auditorium for signs of para-normal activity said that they have even recorded that distinctive voice using EVPs. To collect EVPs, researchers use recording de-vices throughout their investigations, and then they analyze the file for sounds or voices that may emerge from the static in the background.

It's not just performers who share the haunted stage with the ghosts of the Muni; fans get in on the paranormal action. In sev-eral cases, people claim to have heard applause and the excited chatter of what sounds like a bunch of teenyboppers raving over their newest idols. Recording devices picked up some of these auditory effects, too, Muni paranormal experts say.

A tour guide said that while leading people through the auditorium, it's become a natural occurrence for doors to open and close spontaneously—without anyone standing close to them. She said, despite numerous checks and attempts to debunk the phenomena, no one can find a natural explanation of the phenomena. There's no draft. There's no broken door. There are no pranksters nearby.

That activity was confirmed by a group of ghost hunters, who said that while investigating the Muni one team member heard a door slam shut. The ghost hunter said it was no ordinary breeze-driven, door-slamming event—the door was a huge, metal door. It would take more than a breeze to shut it. She left the investigation without an explanation for the door-shutting incident, the ghost hunter added.

It's not just ghost hunters who encounter odd phenomena in the auditorium; musicians report they encounter a chilly reception at the Muni. Not from the fans. They're usually great. They get the cold shoulder—and cold rest of the body—from the spirits that roam the stage at the auditorium.

The musicians say that often when they are playing, they suddenly feel like the temperature drops significantly. They move a little in either direction and they suddenly warm up. They step back to the place where they were just standing—and as quick as a rim shot on the snare, it's cold again. Paranormal experts point out that this is classic spirit activity. When a spirit manifests, it pulls energy from the area, causing the temperature to drop, they say.

Musicians may bear the brunt of the haunting at the Muni, but some people say musicians do most of the haunting at the stadium. Patsy Cline is another one of the star spirits at the Muni.

Paranormal enthusiasts over the years have claimed to have collected enough evidence to prove, at least in their eyes, that the stadium is haunted. The evidence includes snapshots of objects and orbs flitting around the stadium halls and stage. They also have recorded voices of people whispering and chatting. Investigators say these voices may belong to fans and celebrities—Johnny Cash's distinctive voice has been picked up on occasion, for example—who have visited the Muni a long, long time ago. There's even one recording of a ghostly Johnny Cash fan. People who have heard this recording claim to hear a voice say, "I love Johnny Cash," even though no one said this when the recording device was running.

MEMORIAL HALL:
MEMORIES AREN'T THE ONLY THINGS THAT LIVE ON

Memorial Hall, a 3,500-seat auditorium located in downtown Kansas City, Kansas, has played host to some of the music industry's most historic concerts and that includes dozens of America's most important country music acts. But over the years, the building has served as a venue for something else—ghost hunts.

Ghost-hunting teams have traveled to the auditorium to verify the dozens of stories about paranormal activity there. These accounts include tales of deceased workers and music celebrities, including Patsy Cline. Cline gave her last performance at a benefit show there in 1963, two days before her death in an airplane crash.

Since Cline's untimely death, people have sworn they have seen a woman in the building who looks exactly like Cline in her prime. She has been described either as a filmy spirit moving in the far reaches of the hall, or as a completely human-looking female who catches the eye of a visitor and then, as soon as she is recognized, quickly disappears by filtering into the crowd. Staff members have reported coming in contact with Cline, too, usually late at night or early in the morning after all of the concert-goers have gone home. This is offered as evidence that another explanation for the haunting promoted by skeptics—that a lookalike is responsible for the supposed haunting—is extremely unlikely.

One leader of a ghost-hunting group that leads tours of haunted sites in Kansas told a reporter for the *Basehor Sentinel* that Cline's ghost is an example of a residual spirit.

"It's just a residual energy, like a tape being played over and over again," said Beth Cooper, a guide for Ghost Tours of Kansas.

In other words, Cline's ghost may not be trying to reach out to visitors in the hall. The highly charged emotional event—particularly the last performance of her career—may have etched Cline's vivacious spirit right onto the fabric of time and space at the concert hall.

At least Cline has company in the hall. Another ghost is frequently added to the list of possible spooks in Memorial Hall. People report they have seen the spirit of a man appear in the auditorium. Although the details are sketchy and actual evidence of the incident is difficult to find, a rumor—or urban legend—persists that the figure seen in the theater is the spirit of a stagehand who was reportedly electrocuted in the hall sometime during the 1980s.

A ballroom in the building has become a center of paranormal activity. Workers have heard footsteps crossing the floor around them, even though they know they are alone in the building. Music sometimes begins to play, without explanation or, seemingly, a source. Lights outside of the ballroom turn on and off—also by themselves.

These accounts are backed up by paranormal researchers who have gathered evidence in the nearly century-old concert venue. One ghost-hunting team picked up an image of a man on their thermal camera. The figure appeared near the stage—a place that's frequently the site of haunted encounters.

Ghost hunters who use recording devices to pick up voices from discarnate entities also report success at the auditorium. The voice of what sounds to be a woman was picked up in one example of electronic voice phenomena—or EVP, as researchers typically refer to it.

Critics won't be convinced that the scratchy recording of a woman's voice is evidence, but for staff members who have spent time in the wee hours of the morning traipsing through Memorial Hall alone, they don't need critics to tell them what evidence is. They are convinced that there is something strange going on in the auditorium.

THE BIJOU: BOO AT THE BIJOU

For years, country stars and their fans—along with lots of other famous musicians and actors—have streamed into the Bijou Theater, the beautiful and historic theater in Knoxville, Tennessee. When they leave this exceptional piece of Knoxville culture and history, some of them take an extra souvenir with them—ghost stories.

Over the years, the theater has served as everything from a concert hall to an adult movie house. It's been a rocky road for the theater, too, suffering through lots of entertainment ups and downs and economic booms and busts. But the one thing that hasn't changed is that people continually claim to experience paranormal activity at the theater. Now the ghosts almost receive higher billing than the musicians at the Bijou.

A few of the ghosts are so well known that they have nicknames. There's one who most people just refer to as "The Colonel."

Historians say that as Union troops fought to take control of Knoxville, William Sanders, often referred to as "Doc" or Colonel Sanders (the other Colonel Sanders), was shot by a sharpshooter and brought to the Bijou, which was called the Lamar House at the time. Sanders, who had risen to the rank of general during the Civil War, never recovered from his wounds and he died in the house the following day.

His ghost was said to roam around the house and he was often seen and felt in the Bridal Suite, supposedly the very room where he died. When that section of the house was torn down, like any great soldier, Sanders refused to surrender his ground. He reportedly took up residence in the theater. More than a few people have seen a presence in the theater who looks out of place—and out of time. People see a uniformed man walking through the theaters. The colonel gets most of the blame for those sightings.

If the Union commander is still haunting the theater, he isn't the only spirit in the house and, based on the company, he definitely won't be bored in the afterlife there. The ghosts of a few prostitutes—the place was once rumored to be a hangout for ladies of ill repute—are known to haunt the theater. People hear wild party noises—people laughing and otherwise whooping it up—but can't seem to locate the source of the party. These manifestations often occur when the theater is supposed to be empty. But, as we've been finding out, the supernatural world never closes.

Then, there are the ghosts of several famous actors and musicians who have been seen on the stage and in the halls of this historic property. Al Jolson, for example, was one of the leading actors in his day. He apparently loved playing the Bijou in Knoxville, because, according to several reports, he keeps on haunting the place. His ghost—or the spirit of someone who looks just like the *Jazz Singer* star—makes its appearance to staff members and guests on a regular basis.

Some witnesses have described ghosts that float across the floor and ones that even fly above the stage, so it's hard to mistake these spirits for people who just happen to be in the building late at night.

If you don't actually see a spirit in the historic Bijou, there are other ways the spirits manifest. On occasion, you can hear the shuffling of footsteps, like people are heading toward the stage, or maybe leaving during intermission. Doors close by themselves.

For country fans, the Bijou might offer more than just a place to see a great show—it may offer them a glimpse into the great beyond.

PARAMOUNT ART CENTER: ACHY BREAKY HAUNT

In the 1940s, a group of construction workers, who were returning from their lunch break, picked up their hammers and tools to get back to work on what would be a shining showplace of fun and entertainment in Ashland, Kentucky. Something was wrong, though. Maybe it was the creak of planks, or perhaps it was the pendulum-like swing of a shadow sliding along the walls, but for some reason, a worker decided to look up and—to his absolute horror—saw the body of a fellow employee who everyone called Joe swinging from the stage rafters.

No one knows if Joe committed suicide or fell victim to a bizarre accident, but things were never the same in the theater. After the death, the haunting of the Paramount Theater and later, the Paramount Arts Center, began in earnest. Staff members, audience members, and entertainers began to report a string of inexplicable encounters with Paramount Joe, the nickname of the auditorium's ghost-in-residence.

Cold drafts suddenly gust in the theater without any known source—no one opened a door or a window, for instance. Sure, you're thinking, but old buildings are known to have drafts. Okay, then, believers counter, what about the objects that go missing mere seconds after someone has set them down? Happens all the time, you'll counter. Then explain the apparition of a man who has been seen by the most credible witnesses. That's a little more difficult to explain by natural phenomena.

Investigators into the Paramount Arts Center haunting tell us we don't know a lot about Paramount Joe, nor are we likely to find out much about the man behind the ghost. We don't know who he was or why he remains in the center. We do know, however, a couple things. First, despite the terrible death, the ghost is friendly. Second, Paramount Joe loves country music. You can ask Billy Ray Cyrus.

Cyrus was just at the very tip of his meteoric rise when he decided to use the picturesque theater as the perfect backdrop for the video for "Achy Breaky Heart," the song that would send him into country superstardom and help him cross over to pop audiences.

As Cyrus filmed, the staff filled him in about Paramount Joe, and the singer, by all accounts, was really taken by the ghost story. During pauses in the filming of the video, Cyrus would talk to Joe and even ask Joe questions and joke around with the spirit. Sometimes, Cyrus would ask Joe for a little bit of extra assistance as he filmed the video. The two really hit it off—and, later on, Paramount Joe was about to hit back to let everyone know just how tight of a bond existed between him and the singer.

The story goes that once Billy Ray was finished with filming the video the staff asked him to sign some photographs and posters. Cyrus, naturally, agreed. When the country music superstar's career took off, you can bet every single one of those framed photographs appeared in Paramount Arts Center's "Wall of Fame." The framed photographs remained there for years, something that must have made Billy Ray's spirit buddy pretty happy.

Billy Ray even signed some posters for the ladies on the staff, all with a personal inscription. He didn't leave Paramount Joe out, either. The star signed one poster for Paramount Joe with a personal note for the ghost. The ladies put their posters up near their office spaces. Paramount Joe's went on a wall with posters and pictures of other famous artists.

Later, however, the auditorium staff realized they had a problem—a good problem. Over the years, dozens and dozens of celebrities visited the Paramount and signed their own photos for the Wall of Fame. They were literally running out of room. Leadership decided to take some of the Billy Ray Cyrus photos down to make way for the new pictures. The ladies, big fans of Billy Ray, did not want to take down their posters, so everyone agreed that Paramount Joe's poster of the singer had to come down.

Paramount Joe did not take the news well. The morning after the poster went down, the staff members who came into the auditorium first were aghast: each and every picture and poster on the Wall of Fame was scattered along the floor, like someone emphatically, but indignantly, blew them right off of the wall. Glass was shattered. Frames were bent. The level of destruction made some staff members believe that these frames didn't just slip off the wall; they looked as if they were slammed down hard. Really hard. Someone was not happy with the decision to de-Billy Ray the walls. You can bet who the staff blamed.

Paramount Joe is a friendly ghost, but he has his limits. The management also knew he was reasonable and quickly placed the Billy Ray Cyrus poster on the wall in what is now a cafe at the facility.

That seemed to work. There have been no more outbreaks of spirit vandalism against the Wall of Fame artists. But Paramount Joe is still pretty active.

Well Thanks, Joe

Once, a group of employees decided they wanted to explore the basement. The basement was rumored to hold unknown treasures from the auditorium's earlier days. They hoped to find some. In any event, our intrepid explorers opened up the basement door and clicked on the light switch. (At each section, there's a new light switch that illuminates the next section. You have to turn lights on and off at the same switch.)

One staff member, who had been in the basement before and knew where the light switches were located, clicked on the light at the top of the stairs and two other employees walked down the steps. The ghost stories must have been echoing in the back of their minds as the staff members descended that first flight of stairs. Just as the third employee was about to join them, though, the phone rang and he went back to take the call. He said he would be right back, but the coworkers never heard him. The soon-to-be paranormal investigators kept going, either out of bravery—hoping they would run into Paramount Joe—or out of fear, sensing that the quicker they entered, the quicker they could depart.

They moved on to the next section and called out to their coworker to hit the switch to turn on the lights. And just like that, the light was switched on. Once the employees were finished, they returned and saw that their coworker was still at the top of the stairs. He wasn't right behind them as they thought. They thanked him, however, for turning on the lights.

The third coworker was confused. He told them that, because the phone call was more involved than he thought, he didn't return to turn on the lights. In fact, he believed his coworkers were still waiting for him to return. He had no idea that they were pressing on into the dark and cavernous—and apparently haunted—basement. They took him back to the basement and, sure enough, whoever turned the lights on so graciously for the staff, turned them right back off again.

The three coworkers who just recorded another brush with the paranormal at the Paramount stood in stunned silence for a moment, until one yelled, "Well thanks, Joe."

CHAPTER 10

COUNTRY SPIRITS: BARS, CLUBS, TAVERNS, AND HONKY-TONKS

Country music is not written and performed exclusively for knocking a few back and packing the dance floor at the local honky-tonk, but the music sure takes on a life of its own when it is performed at those local watering holes. Country fans aren't the only ones who enjoy the lively environment of country-music friendly bars, clubs, taverns, and honky-tonks.

Paranormal experts and music fans alike say these spaces harbor more than liquid spirits, they hold lost spirits—ghosts of former owners and patrons—along with other wandering souls who became attached to the establishments in either their former lives or current afterlife journey.

Most of these spirits are not harmful. They, in fact, can be friendly. But some of the most dangerous ghosts of country music are known to haunt bars and honky-tonks. One of the most famous—and scariest—stories of ghostly and ghastly paranormal interactions will be up first when we visit arguably the world's most haunted country music bar—Bobby Mackey's Music World.

BOBBY MACKEY'S MUSIC WORLD: ONE HAUNTED HONKY-TONK

When country music star Bobby Mackey bought a bar in Wilder, Kentucky, he expected some rough-and-tumble guests. After all, what would a honky-tonk be without a few knock-down, drag-outs every now and then. And the fact that the bar was based in "Wilder," should have been a clue that things could get a little out-of-hand in this corner of Kentucky.

He just had no idea that some of those rough-and-tumble guests looking for a fight would be dead.

Bobby Mackey's Music World is one of the most haunted locations in country music's vast paranormal landscape. The haunting of this establishment has been investigated on television and explored in books. Documentary filmmakers and television news crews continue to visit Bobby Mackey's to tell and retell the story of the haunting.

On paper and on film, Bobby Mackey's doesn't look like your typical haunted property. In fact, it looks like a normal bar and restaurant located on the gentle lapping shores of the Licking River. Maybe that's why Mackey didn't suspect anything back in the late 1970s when he signed his name to the bottom line of the agreement to purchase the bar.

Within days, though, the country star and one time paranormal skeptic said events began to happen to eventually convince him that not only did the supernatural exist, but that there was something inexplicable happening in his new investment. Workers who were preparing the bar for opening noticed that the lights turned on and off by themselves. Believing the light show was nothing more than wiring problems, they were able to laugh off the phenomenon. But, as we'll discover in a later chapter on haunted jukeboxes, when an unplugged jukebox began to play by itself, Mackey and his employees grew more suspicious. You can't blame the wiring when the thing isn't plugged in, after all.

The activity was weird but harmless, at least at the beginning. Mackey and his family were just receiving a glimpse of the supernatural crowd that had packed his bar. More reports about tangles with ghosts began to roll in. These spirits were highly interactive—some paranormal investigators call them "entities." The ghosts didn't seem like they were great company. Reliable witnesses claimed that an unseen force shoved them. In fact, Mackey's wife, Janet, swore on an affidavit that she was thrown down a set of steps. Others said they were pinched and punched, still other witnesses said they were slapped. In interviews, Mackey said he thought about selling the haunted enterprise, but he had sunk all of his savings into the establishment. He was too invested in the place. There was no turning back.

Over the years, the owner's investigations, as well as information gathered from some of the ghost hunters and sensitives that Mackey and his wife brought in, began to unravel the bar's disturbing history and revealed that an extensive list of spirits frequented the bar.

Originally, the bar was a slaughterhouse and there are those who have suggested that this bloodletting attracted malevolent spirits—human and otherwise. Folklorists say that groups affiliated with satanic or dark magic rites once performed their rituals in the slaughterhouse because of the copious quantities of blood for their spells and curses. However, there's no historical evidence that the spot was used as a regular meeting site for satanic worship.

As if its reputation as a convention center for budding evil wizards wasn't enough, the building was rumored to be the scene of a grisly murder and the victim may still haunt the place. There are a few variations of the story, but one of the most popular—which is a mix of both fact and folklore—goes like this:

A young woman named Pearl Bryan met up with two unsavory characters—Alonzo Walling and Scott Jackson—in early February 1896. Townsfolk at the time suspected Walling and Jackson of being associated with the satanic cult that met in the slaughterhouse. Until now, the animal sacrifices were enough to please the dark lord, but he apparently wanted more. Bryan was lured into the slaughterhouse and killed. According to folklore, while police found the body, they never recovered the poor woman's head. Jackson and Walling were quickly apprehended and, although they were offered a lesser sentence of life in prison to disclose the whereabouts of the victim's head, they never did. According to some tales, the murderers were afraid of incurring the wrath of Satan for revealing the location of the sacrifice.

Opting out of the plea deal, the men were convicted of murder and sentenced to death.

Over time, residents spun a tale that indicated the two men threw the head down the slaughterhouse well as part of a ritual to turn the chasm into a gateway to Hell. Experts on the case, as we'll soon find out, say there is no evidence that a head was tossed into the well. (But it still makes a pretty good cover story for the mysterious goings-on at the bar, right?)

Another bit of folklore says that a curse is behind the haunting. Witnesses report that as Walling stepped to the gallows, he eyed those who had gathered to see his execution and those who had condemned him to death. He then spoke his last words—he cursed all of them and vowed to return from the grave and haunt them forever.

Maybe the incidents at Mackey's are related to Walling's curse. It does seem that while most of the country music ghosts that we've talked about in this book are good spirits—although, granted, they too can be a little creepy—the ghosts at Bobby Mackey's place are badasses, even compared to the occasional living badasses who frequent honky-tonks. There's one spirit that witnesses have seen behind the bar—he looks mean and not someone you would want to tangle with. People get a distinctly bad vibe about this ghost, speculating that he's the one who is responsible for many of the negative paranormal interactions with the owner, employees, and patrons. Most bet this is the ghost of the murderous Walling.

Walling may have paranormal company, including one apparition that might be the murderer's victim, though she has a head. People have reported seeing a sad-looking young woman suddenly appear and then just as suddenly disappear. Witnesses say the apparition is nearly see-through, but the apparition creates concrete emotions. Most people who have had a run-in with this spirit say they will be forever haunted by the sad expression on the woman's face.

The female ghost was one of the first spirits to appear to the new owners, according to several sources. During an initial tour of the building, Bobby and Janet made their way through the building. Strangely, the couple watched as a large metal door opened on its own. It was an unwelcoming welcome for the future investors of the property. Undeterred, the couple slid through the now half-opened door and Bobby clambered onto the stage. Looking into the now deserted and dusty bar, Bobby imagined all the chairs filled with people and all the tables filled with drinks and food. While he saw this in his mind's eye, something caught his attention. A woman with a long white gown and long light brown hair was staring back at him from the dance floor!

He called out to the shape, but she disappeared. Knowing that he was lost in thought at the time of the sighting, Bobby told Janet the woman was just a figment of his imagination, maybe a trick of the shadows that danced in the dark, empty room. Janet wasn't so sure, and she became immediately fearful and suspicious. As the owners became more immersed in their new investment, the spirits seemed to take a more active interest in the owners. The darker spirit—or spirits—that reside in the building took pleasure in tormenting Janet. Once while she was cleaning and helping prepare for the club's opening, she began to feel overheated. Since Janet was pregnant at the time, she quickly attributed it to just a rush of hormones. She decided, just to be safe, that it was time to take a break. As Janet walked through the club, she was seized with a chill that was almost paralyzing. Goosebumps formed on her body. Despite being drenched in sweat just moments before, she had never felt this cold. Janet said she heard a nearly inaudible whisper, but she couldn't make out the words. It was unsettling—evil.

In addition to these ghost sightings—and a few ghost shoves—people have claimed to have seen the ghost of a headless woman walking through a crowd of revelers at the club. A ghost dog and a man with a handlebar mustache have also been seen, according to witness testimonies.

There was another rumor that a pregnant woman committed suicide in the club. She was a dancer named Johanna. The story later became the subject of one of Bobby's songs. Urban legend or not, lots of people suggest that it's not a coincidence that Bobby's pregnant wife established some sort of spiritual connection with the ghost of the ill-fated pregnant dancer.

The late Carl Lawson, one of the bar's first employees, wasn't just tormented; he was possessed, according to his own account. He served as the caretaker and was more exposed to the supernatural forces that gripped the premises because he also lived in an apartment above the club. On several occasions, Lawson said spirits assaulted him.

Eventually, Lawson began to believe he was possessed. He became self-destructive and continually entertained evil thoughts. His friends and coworkers began to notice the transformation, especially since Lawson's normal disposition was helpful and friendly. The disruption became so bad that—during his more lucid moments—he agreed to undergo an exorcism. The grueling, six-hour ceremony was held in the deep recesses of the building, a section that has—maybe not coincidentally—been torn down. During the exorcism, the spirit that possessed Lawson fought with the preacher performing the rite, physically and verbally. He also began to speak in German and Latin, two languages Lawson swore he did not know.

Lawson's experiences had far-reaching impact for his best friend, Mackey. The club owner had plans to tear down the building. Although, for the most part, he dismissed the paranormal experiences of his employees and family members, reports are that the videotaped exorcism of his caretaker made him reconsider. Mackey wanted to build a new club on a nearby plot of land. The spirits had other plans. While walking through his club, a chunk of the ceiling fell on him as he was talking about the pending demolition. Then, a six-inch-wide, sixty-foot-deep crack spread from the original property to the site of the new club. The crack made the new club a financial impossibility. Mackey and the engineers probably couldn't help but notice that the crack originated at the well—the epicenter of the haunting.

Douglas Hensley, who has written extensively about the haunting and wrote a book on it, called *Hell's Gate*, said there are no shortages of witnesses who are willing to tell their stories of paranormal encounters in the bar. Along with Janet, nearly thirty people have signed off on sworn affidavits on the supernatural activity that they saw. Before you think that this is just a list of Mackey's regulars who may have tossed back one too many shots, or one too many falls from the electronic bull, these witnesses come from a cross-section of society, including Mackey's patrons and employees, but also clergy and police.

The Haunting Continues

One of country music's most active hauntings shows no signs of taking a break, according to the leader of a paranormal group that has been assigned to lead tours of the club.

Laura Roland, an investigator and cofounder of Gatekeeper Paranormal, has been giving tours and collecting evidence at Bobby Mackey's Music World since July 2014. The team is now the official paranormal team at the bar. And they are convinced there is something paranormal going on. The range of supernatural activity experienced by the team goes from the benign to the somewhat threatening, although she doesn't believe that there's anything demonic going on in the site.

"We have captured several EVPs, we have had pebbles thrown, pieces of glass thrown—from broken bottles in the basement," Roland reports in an email interview. "We've been touched, seen shadows and blue balls of light, and heard many footsteps and knocking."

While some of the activity does seem aggressive, Roland doesn't believe that demons or any type of malicious entity is causing the activity. It may just be a spirit's way of saying hello.

"Even though rocks and pieces of glass have been thrown, I don't consider that to be necessarily negative," she writes. "It could just be the only way the entity can communicate or try to get us to notice he/she is there."

It might not be a demon, but spirits in the dwelling are no one to be trifled with, she warns. A few people have reported being hit and scratched after they tried provoking spirits. Giving a rowdy ghost hunter his or her just deserts isn't necessarily a sign of demonic activity either, the paranormal researcher said.

At one time or another, nearly all of the team members have felt a heavy presence in the building, one that made them feel unwelcome.

Roland says: "Having said all that … there have been times for each of us that we have walked in the building alone and turned around and walked right back out to wait for our tour group. It's hard to explain, but sometimes there is just a feeling in the building that is unwelcoming. It doesn't happen every time we go in. Each of us has spent time alone in the building and had nothing happen. But sometimes it's just creepy. Could it be overactive imaginations? Sure. But maybe not."

The group of researchers collected several theories about what is haunting the property—and it could be more than one ghost, they add. The site is the center of and near to several violent incidents that may lie at the root of the paranormal occurrences. For instance, it was a hotbed for gangster activity in the 1940s and 1950s and there were bar fights—some of them fatal—when the location was a Hard Rock Cafe in the early 1970s, according to the researchers. There are other tragedies—a fatal car crash just a mile away and the use of the bar's dance floor as a temporary morgue after a devastating fire—that experts list as reasons for the haunted activity.

Bobby Mackey's Music World may not so much have ghosts, but attract them. Roland reports that paranormal theorists have investigated whether geological anomalies might have something to do with the activity. There's a layer of limestone and running water that may serve as a conduit—a haunted highway—of sorts for these roadhouse spirits. Investigators also report naturally high electromagnetic field (EMF) readings at the site, often an indicator for supernatural goings-on.

When the team gives tours, members use some of their research to shed light on the folklore that revolves around that haunting at the bar. For instance, there's no historical evidence that Johanna existed. The murder most likely did not occur at the site, either. The two murderers may have passed by the site when they were trying to get rid of the body, but actually disposed of it a few miles away, the team members report.

A TOAST TO NASHVILLE'S GHOSTS: MUSIC CITY'S HAUNTED BARS AND CLUBS

While auditoriums, like the Ryman, and grand stages, like those at Opryland, represent the pinnacle of country music success in Nashville, most of the young up-and-comers, the fading stars, the has-beens, and the never-weres spend every night building—or recapturing—an audience on the intimate stages of the city's thriving bars, clubs, and restaurants.

It's on these boulevards that meet at the corner of fulfilled wishes and broken dreams that you'll find some of country music's most haunted tales. They are stories about the spirits of people who made it, and people who lost it, while pursuing their dreams of country music stardom. You'll also find tales of lost loves and lost lives, and hints of Nashville's violent past, a past full of conflict and war, greed and hunger.

Tootsie's Orchid Lounge

We'll start at one of the most famous clubs in Nashville and, perhaps, the most famous in haunted country music history—Tootsie's Orchid Lounge.

Spirits—the ones on tap and in the bottles—attracted the stars headlining at the nearby Ryman Auditorium to walk around the corner to Tootsie's Orchid Lounge. Some of those performers, though, are now spirits of a different sort, spirits who are attracting a following of their own from ghost hunters and people who are interested in what lies beyond in the afterworld.

Tootsie's, a country music drinking tradition, began in the early 1960s when Tootsie Bess bought a bar named Mom's. The "orchid" part of the title was added when a painter slapped a coat of purple on the bar—a total surprise to Tootsie. But, like everything, the bar owner rolled with the strange twist of fate.

Tootsie's stage welcomed acts like Kris Kristofferson, Faron Young, Willie Nelson, Tom T. Hall, Hank Cochran, Mel Tillis, Roger Miller, Webb Pierce, Waylon Jennings, Patsy Cline, and many more. Lots of fortunes began here and lots of careers were made here. Willie Nelson got his first songwriting gig after singing at Tootsie's.

But Tootsie also knew that there were broken dreams littered along the alley between the Ryman and her bar. People used to see her hand five or ten bucks to down-on-their-luck performers.

When Tootsie died in 1978, country music's brightest luminaries, like Roy Acuff and Tom T. Hall, among other customers, showed up at the funeral to bid one of their favorite supporters so long. Country star Connie Smith sang hymns at the funeral.

Tootsie's generous spirit is still felt in the club today, a few patrons say. They say they have the distinct impression that she is still watching over her beloved bar. For instance, whenever there's a band or solo artist performing on stage, you'll know that Tootsie approves right away if her ghost appears at the end of the bar. Others say that this ghost isn't Tootsie, it's Patsy Cline who is lending her support to the new burgeoning stars of country. Cline, as we discussed, held forth at Tootsie's and never let the good old boys club of country music keep her from having a good time. Patrons remember Cline knocking a few back with the boys and cracking jokes with the best of them.

But Patsy and Tootsie are not the only spirits in the house, they are joined by at least one other country legend that we've talked about a lot in this book: the ole rambling spirit, Hank Williams.

Like some of the other spots where Williams has revealed his presence in Nashville, lots of witnesses claim to see the misty yet easily discernible figure of the lanky musical rebel perched on the barstool. In most cases, ghosts tend to be camera shy, but at Tootsie's, Williams seems relaxed and ready for fans. Years ago, a photo of the odd apparition at Tootsie's was reportedly passed around and featured in the media. Some say that the photo showed the ghost of Hank Williams. Other times, people have seen a guy who looks just like Hank Williams suddenly appear in a crowd at the club—and then, after a few blinks to check their vision—they say he simply vanishes. His spirit has also been seen in the alley that connects the Ryman with the lounge. It was a trek he knew well, from most accounts.

Williams, that rambling spirit, likes to stretch his legs a bit. People have seen Williams—dressed in slacks, cowboy boots, and a long-sleeved white shirt—walking the alley that leads from the Ryman to Tootsie's. Witnesses say the ghost makes eye contact, nods his head, and then disappears.

Paranormal researchers aren't sure who to attribute some of the other phenomena that folks have witnessed in this super-spirited lounge. Odd noises are reported and there are shadowy figures that dart through the dark halls and around the stages in Tootsie's. Whether this activity is related to the ghosts of Tootsie or Williams—or any of the other thousands of souls who passed through the purple-encrusted doors of the establishment—we may never know.

Flying Saucer

It's not little green men that people need to look out for when they head to the Flying Saucer Draught Emporium—one of

Nashville's favorite nightspots; it's the ghost of an old man and a whole flask full of strange and supernatural activity that they must be wary of. But, by all accounts, the ghosts and the still-living patrons, staff, performers, and bar owners have reached a kind of peace with each other, even, it seems, embracing the presence of each other.

The bar, located on Tenth Avenue in Nashville, is near the center of Music City's wild action, but it is right smack dab in an epicenter of even wilder supernatural action. After experiencing weird phenomena for years in the bar, management called in a group of expert ghost hunters, who quickly scheduled an investigation.

The management team filled in the paranormal investigators on the details of the activity. The list was lengthy. While people have experienced supernatural phenomena throughout the bar, it's the billiard room that gets the most supernatural attention. The coin slots that feed quarters into the pool tables move in and out—on their own. Billiard balls slide across their table suddenly, too. You could blame that on uneven tables or floor, but objects don't have to be on the billiard table in that room to slide around. The cue sticks fall, drinks topple off of tables, and chairs move across the floor, all as horrified patrons watch in open-mouth shock.

Television sets in the billiard room have another type of remote control, as in they are remotely controlled by unseen spiritual entities. The sets turn on and off and then change stations. The sets suddenly mute, or the volume inexplicably blares.

The most convincing piece of evidence came from members of the bar's cleaning crew who say they often encounter the ghost of an old man walking around the bar. Other people have said they looked into the mirrors at the bar and saw not just their own reflection, but they also see an apparition whose icy eyes stare right back at them.

From all indications, the investigation was eventful to say the least. A manager of the Flying Saucer went along with the paranormal investigators. At one stage, as the manager held on to a digital thermometer, an investigator asked the spirit to make the temperature drop to signal its presence. The manager said they heard someone mumble and clearly heard the word, "try." Then the thermometer showed that the temperature had dropped by ten degrees. It's important to note that, according to the testimony of the manager, the voice they heard was not a type of electronic voice phenomena, where people claim to hear words in the static of a recording device that they either interpret or misinterpret as voices and words. They heard an actual disembodied voice.

Experts on this haunting say the most likely reason for the activity at the Flying Saucer is because the building was once part of Nashville's famous train station, Union Station. The train station was the scene of numerous emotional homecomings. Soldiers returning from war would meet their loved ones in the station. Fans could go to Union Station to get a glimpse of their favorite country stars heading out or coming back from tours and performances, too. But there were other much more desperate reunions in the train station. In fact, the billiard room may be placed right where the baggage claim area of the notoriously haunted train station was once situated. In the aftermath of a horrible train wreck in the 1900s, local historians say the baggage area became an impromptu morgue.

The paranormal experts suggested that all of these highly-charged emotions—the good and the bad—have been embedded into the space that is now the billiard room. The apparitions and the odd events that witnesses have reported over the years are just a manifestation of that spiritual energy that became entwined in one of Nashville's favorite bars.

Hermitage Cafe

Nashville is a town of big dreams and sometimes, it's a town of big broken dreams. All those dreamers—big and broken and everywhere in between—usually find themselves at one time or another at the Hermitage Cafe in downtown Nashville. Open all night, the restaurant attracts a diverse group of Nashville's nightlife dwellers.

They are joined by the ultimate nightlife dweller—a ghost.

According to local historians, Shields Taylor owned the cafe until his death and then his wife took over. There are lots of patrons and workers at the restaurant who think that Taylor never left. The ghostly occurrences include a variety of poltergeist-like effects—moving objects and misplaced items—along with a few incidents of direct physical interventions by an invisible force. Some of the run-ins with the ghost are more violent than others, as we will discover.

Employees talk a lot about the pots and pans that typically hang peacefully in the kitchen suddenly start clanging together. Witnesses have also watched or listened to the doors shake violently, as if an intruder is entering. When they investigate, though, no one is there. Inexplicable knocking noises erupt throughout the cafe. Again, when people try to investigate, they are hard pressed to determine the source.

Whatever is haunting the cafe gets up-close and personal with patrons. Women say they have had their hair touched. It feels like a quick gust of wind blew their hair, they say. Guys, on the other hand, have felt more than a gentle hair play; a few male patrons say they were shoved.

People who are familiar with the haunting blame Taylor because the restaurant was pretty quiet, at least supernaturally speaking, until the former owner died. After that, people began to notice the paranormal outbreaks. Most long-time customers just put two and two together and agree that Taylor is the one haunting the site. Most of the phenomena is harmless, they add, making it seem more like the former owner just wants to make his presence known every once and awhile.

The Museum Club: The Supernatural on Display

Located in Flagstaff, Arizona, along the musically historic Route 66, the Museum Club is one of the region's favorite country and western bars and, like the great country music songs that have filled the halls of this club over the past few decades, the club has been the scene of great joy and gut-wrenching tragedy. If you think that sounds like the perfect formula for a haunted country music club, you are absolutely right. The Museum Club is one of the most paranormally active country music bars in the nation.

Apparitions are spotted routinely in the building. Other witnesses report much more physically intimidating—and much more terrifying—spirit encounters.

Experts trace the origin of the haunting to the early 1960s when Don Scott, more famously known as the steel guitar player for Bob Wills and His Texas Playboys, bought the joint. They say that the musician stumbled onto what was billed as "the biggest log cabin in Arizona." It's hard to say what Scott saw in the place. It definitely had fallen on hard times. During its three decades or so of existence, the building served as a museum, a nightclub, a taxidermist shop, a trading post, and pretty much everything in between.

But Scott had an idea—and the connections to pull it off. His idea was to turn it into a successful country and western dance hall. As one of country music's luminaries, he had the contacts to fill the club with acts, he figured, and the customers would follow. It worked.

His fellow musicians—people like Waylon Jennings, Willie Nelson, and Bob Wills himself—signed up to perform at the club, and the fans nearly busted down the doors to see them. The club became one of the most important stops on the "western swing" circuit. (The western part of "country and western" refers to western swing music, a jazz-influence genre of country music with an up-tempo and backed by mostly stringed instruments.)

Pretty soon, aspiring country musicians would make sure they booked a gig at the Museum Club as they made that well-trodden hopeful trek across the country, from Nashville to California. But it wasn't just up-and-comers who came to the club. Sometimes, already established acts would pay a visit. Barbara Mandrell came into the Museum Club once and then jumped up on stage for an impromptu set. That happened lots of times—famous celebrities loved to perform these types of spontaneous informal sets at the club.

Don, whom everyone called "Pappy," and his wife, Thorna, lived in an apartment above the club. Their lives literally revolved around the club. However, things were going so well that nobody saw the dark clouds on the horizon. The club's demise began early one morning in 1973 when the couple was cleaning up and preparing to close after yet another successful night. Thorna finished up and was climbing the stairs to the couple's apartment when, as she reached the top of the stairs, she tripped and fell. The accident broke her neck.

While she hovered between life and death in the hospital, Pappy was clearly distraught. After a few weeks, Thorna died. The death was too much for Pappy to take and although he tried to go on with his life, the loss of his wife caused him to slip into a deep depression. In 1975, Pappy was found dead in front of the fireplace, according to several sources.

Experts on the haunting now say that the property has been unsettled since those two tragic events. Numerous reports of supernatural activity have piled in, even as the new management has maintained the club's position as a hot spot for country acts and great country music.

Some of the activity is benign and a little easier to explain away as unusual, but completely natural phenomena. For instance, that cool breeze across the neck that some patrons complain about. That could just be a draft. It's a relatively old building and older places tend to have drafts. You can try to tell that to someone who has experienced the draft, but they might not fully accept your explanation. When witnesses feel that cold breeze, they say there is just something in the air—a chill, or an electric field—that makes them think this is more than just a crack in the paneling, or a draft from a window.

Other activity is harder to explain. For example, people hear the creak of the floorboards. While random board creaks and cracks are normal, witnesses say they can detect a pattern. The witnesses say it sounds like someone is walking toward them, or away from them, but that someone just happens to be invisible. There are others who say they can hear not squeaks and creaks of wooden boards, but definite footsteps.

Customers and workers have also reported that lights flicker in certain rooms, while, simultaneously, the lights remain steady in other parts of the club. But forget the electromagnetic displays for a second, there are actually stories that blazes can erupt in the fireplace all by themselves. In a more chilling display of occult power, chairs will rock on their own.

Skeptics have explanations for most of these events—loose wiring, the settling of an old building, etc.—but these same cynics of the supernatural struggle to explain the spirit of a woman that has been seen in the club. She most often appears in the back stairway and back bar, but has also shown up in booths situated in the darker areas of the bar.

The woman has such a physical appearance that customers often mistake her for a bartender and they order a drink. But when they look back again to pick up their drink, she's gone. When the befuddled patron explains to a (living) employee what happened and start to describe the encounter, they are met with a knowing look and a weird reply: the bartender was the ghost of former owner Thorna Scott. Often an employee will show the witnesses a picture of the former owner and they'll say that the woman in the picture is the person they saw in the bar. For effect, the staff member will add that the woman passed away decades ago.

You Only Need to Fear the Living. Really?

Not all encounters are this tame. One ghost apparently has an ironic streak as our next story demonstrates. One man who rented the upstairs apartment said the ghost of a woman jumped on his chest and pinned him to the floor. The ghost then told the man, "You only need to fear the living."

The tenant did not take the apparition's advice, however. As soon as the ghost faded from his view, the man didn't even bother exiting through the door. He jumped up, dove out the window, and ran along the roof to safety.

He never came back. Can you blame him?

A bartender claimed that she, too, had felt the presence of the bar's ghost, although, thankfully, the spirit didn't feel the need to jump on her chest to get the message across. She said that she was starting her shift when she noticed that the bar was completely disorganized. Beer bottles had been moved out of their correct spots and liquor bottles were tipped over. She found that something moved the drink mixes. With no practical jokers around to fess up to the prank, the bartender pointed her finger of blame squarely on the spirits of the former owners, the Scotts.

The haunting of the Museum Club spans decades, but the phenomena continue, as recent reports indicate. One recent story is that an employee watched as the lights in the apartment were turning on and off. The typical knee-jerk skeptical response to this phenomena—that there is an electrical problem in the old apartment—was immediately taken off the table. Power to the apartment had been completely shut off. The employee revealed that the mystery was never solved.

Recently, one employee of the Museum Club reported that though the power in the upstairs floor has been shut off, the lights have been coming on more and more often. Others have reported also seeing the lights from the street while driving by late at night.

The mysteries—just like the great country music—keeps on coming at the Museum Club, it seems.

CHAPTER 11

SUPERNATURAL STUDIOS AND RECORD COMPANY HEADQUARTERS

Studios are where musicians turn inspiration into revelation. Literally, these are places where spirit is created and preserved. It's not just their musical inspiration that is maintained for posterity. Some believe that these hit factories are also capable of retaining paranormal forces.

You won't have to tell that to people who have experienced strange, inexplicable activity while recording or assisting at these studios.

In our next section, we will visit some of country music's most famous recording studios. They are also some of country music's famously haunted recording studios. Some are haunted by multiple ghosts, according to experts. Others are haunted by multiple gold and platinum award-winning artists, like the King himself—Elvis Presley.

Up first, though, we will hear the creepy backstory behind the haunting at one of Nashville's greatest star-making machines— Capitol Records.

CAPITOL RECORDS: SPECTRE CHECK ON MIC ONE

Historians indicate that the site where Capitol Records's world famous Nashville studios rests was developed while country music was just a bunch of people picking guitars and banjos on porches and singing in rural churches. Country music and Capitol Records grew up together in Nashville, you might say, and, over time, a parade of country and western careers were made and shepherded into celebrity status right there at Capitol Records, including some supernovas of the country music universe.

Tourists hoping to catch a glimpse of a ghost in Nashville now believe that the studio is prime ghost hunting ground. Most trace the paranormal problems on the property well back into distant Nashville history. According to the legend, a mansion was built on the spot at the turn of the twentieth century. By all accounts it was magnificent. But, despite the ostentatious new digs, the owner of the mansion and his two daughters were never accepted into Nashville's high society. In the South, there's a difference between new wealth and old wealth. And new wealth just doesn't fit in.

Eventually, the father died and left the property to his daughters. Why the daughters never found husbands is a subject of a lot of speculation—gossipy speculation. Some say they were perfectly happy without men in their lives. Others suggest that the public shunning of the family by the social elites ensured the poor girls would live and die as spinsters. Those who believe the family was unhappy say that's the reason that the home—and now the property itself—is haunted. When the mansion was torn down to make way for the new building that included office space for Capitol Records, the hauntings commenced in earnest.

At night, or early in the morning, when the building was otherwise still and quiet, employees who were alone in the building—especially those unlucky enough to be working on the building's eleventh floor, the center of the haunting—would swear that they heard footsteps trudging down the halls. The footfalls were distinctly human, they said. But as the workers followed the sound to its origin, they discovered nothing. Nada. Nobody.

Just an empty hall.

Other witnesses haven't just heard manifestations of the spirit world, they have actually seen the effects. Several stories have circulated of people watching doors slowly and silently close on their own, without anyone even close to them. Subsequent investigations and attempts to replicate the weird phenomena suggest that a mechanical cause—an uneven floor, a loose door, etc.—are not the cause of the problem. Even more annoying for workers in the building: the doors lock automatically, often at the worst possible times. The building doesn't use electronic switches, either, so it's not a case of bad wiring or an electrical short. These are manual locks, reports indicate. Employees and folks who have heard about the haunting know who's to blame: the ghost.

The ghost, or ghosts, announce their presence in other ways. They like to mess with electronic devices, wreaking all sorts of havoc for employees trying to work on their computers, make a phone call, or watch television. Of course, when your business is making music, fiddling with electronic gear is a surefire way to attract attention.

Anecdotally, the word has spread that people have seen the actual ghosts involved in the haunting. Witnesses claim to have seen two women in the building when the building should be vacant. Could they just be guests, or unaccounted for staff members? Could be. Or they could be the ghosts of two lonely residents of the property—two ghosts who intend on being ghosts for a very long time to come.

RCA STUDIOS:
DOES IT STAND FOR REALLY CRAZY ACTIVITY?

There are a lot of ghosts who are rumored to be lurking in the shadows and cowering in the corners of RCA's historic studio in Nashville.

Some of the spectral suspects are just the ghosts of normal people, experts on the haunting say. Other sources indicate it is the long-dead country musicians who once filled the studios of this building who are coming back to lay down one more track. In fact, a lot of people think that Elvis is haunting the Nashville landmark. It's a tourist twofer: you get to see a ghost and you get to see Elvis. But be careful what you wish for. The spooky activity in this building can sometimes shake even the most dedicated fan of country music.

Some of the stories that have trickled out of this one-time hit-making factory—RCA has long since transferred recording operations from the building—include tales of poltergeist-like activity and odd electromagnetic effects. One of the most famous anecdotes about the paranormal happenings in the studio is told by workers and production assistants in the television studio that the building once housed. They swear that every time someone says, "Elvis," weird things happened. Lights would blow up. Ladders would topple over. Strange noises could be heard.

On a few occasions, when the television crews would attempt to record in the building, weird noises would leak through. The staff didn't hear the sounds when they were recording, only when they listened to the playback. The crew was stumped. Wouldn't a former recording studio be a perfect place to record? They called in engineers and they, too, had no rational reason for the recording snafus. Some thought it was the spirit of Elvis trying to communicate from the other side. In fact, there were no natural explanations for any of the activity in Elvis's former—or not so former—haunt.

It's hard to say who is haunting the studio, though. That's the real mystery of the haunting. After all, tons of artists who recorded here—Hank Snow, Jim Reeves, Roy Orbison, and Roger Miller, to name a few—have passed on and might want to return to the scene of what was possibly the highest point of their careers.

But most experts on Nashville paranormal keep coming back to their number one suspect: Elvis. After all, some of the most supercharged events—the recording of "Heartbreak Hotel" comes to mind—of the King's supercharged career started right in that studio. That powerful psychic energy still reverberates in the studio, these theorists suggest.

If you ever take a peanut butter and banana sandwich to the studio and it disappears, well, then we'll know for sure.

BENNETT HOUSE (BAGBEY HOUSE): FROM CIVIL WAR SPIRITS TO STUDIO SPIRITS

The famous country musicians who wandered in and out of the Bennett House—one of Franklin, Tennessee's most storied mansions and, at one time, one of country music's most successful hit-making studios—were all taken in by the charm of the home's elegance. But you have to wonder if some of those country stars couldn't wait to get out of the studio. After all, they knew that while recording there might mean a sure hit record, it might also mean running into a ghost.

The Bennett House, according to experts on the paranormal activity in the region, is one of the most haunted sites in Franklin, Tennessee. And Franklin, a town just south of Nashville, is one of the most haunted spots in Tennessee, if not the country.

Now called the Bagbey House, the building's unique history—it's been the home of a Confederate war hero, a recording studio, and an antique store during its 100-plus years of existence—may explain some of the spooky activity. When it comes to identifying the spirit suspects in the house, the phantasm's finger usually points to Walter James Bennett, a Confederate soldier who served on the staff of Major General William Whiting.

Once Confederate shells started to land on Union-held Fort Sumter, Bennett signed up to serve in Company B of the 2nd Mississippi Infantry. His service during the battles in and around Virginia brought him to the attention of General Whiting, who took the soldier on as a staff member and personal secretary.

The war did not end so well for Captain Bennett. He was captured and held prisoner of war in Fort Donelson until 1865, according to family history. The fort where Bennett languished was the scene of a bloody battle. This leads paranormal experts to suggest that the psychic scars from the war followed the captain through his life and remain in his manor. There are other theories, though. In addition to Bennett's spirit, a group of Civil War soldiers who once found temporary rest on the home's spacious and shady porch while marching to battle may have found eternal rest on the premises. Perhaps they are haunting the mansion.

Other people familiar with the haunting at Bennett's house claim that it isn't the house that's haunted. (Well, it isn't *just* the house that's haunted.) The whole dang town of Franklin is haunted. A bloody Civil War battle—the same one that turned the Bennett mansion into a rest stop for the weary Confederate troops—consumed the whole town and may have populated the town's houses, businesses, and streets with a permanent citizenry full of spirits.

In the 1980s, however, the haunted home in this haunted town found a new use. It was converted into a music studio. Norbert Putnam, a top-notch record producer, opened the first studio in the mansion, calling it the Bennett House Studio. Later, multiple Grammy Award-winning producer Keith Thomas took over and expanded the recording facilities. He continued the string of hits to come from the Franklin-based recording facility. Country artists who recorded there included Vince Gill, Kris Kristofferson, Faith Hill, Wynonna Judd, and Trace Adkins. Amy Grant, Vanessa Williams, Jimmy Buffett, Whitney Houston, and Gladys Knight also laid down tracks in the spirit-filled studio.

Strategically located near Nashville, the studio started to make a name for itself among musicians—particularly country musicians—who were looking for new environs to record, but at a site that wasn't too far from country music's main hub. Paranormally speaking, the studio made a name for itself in another way. These musicians and studio workers also began to spread stories of inexplicable activity.

Sometimes, late at night, or early in the morning, while musicians and engineers toiled in the studio, they claimed to hear odd eruptions of thumps and bumps. At other times, the noises were not as random and clearly sounded like a person was walking around upstairs, even when they knew there was no one else in the house. People taking pictures in the building, which is now a major draw for antique lovers, say they can see anomalous shapes and lights appear in their photographs—shapes and lights that weren't there when they took the picture and ones that can't be easily explained as either natural or electronic effects.

William Bagbey, who runs Bagbey House Antiques and Interiors, told reporters he's heard the noises and believes the Confederate captain isn't shy about being photographed.

"Every now and then we can still hear Mr. Bennett walking around upstairs, or see him in pictures we take of the staircase," Bagbey told the *Williamson Herald*. "It's pretty spooky."

It's not just the captain that interrupted recording sessions. Musicians said they heard children laughing in the house. In nearly all those cases, there were no children on the property at the time—and they certainly wouldn't be allowed to interrupt these sessions where time is literally money. They also claim to hear kids running through the house. The rambunctious rumbling of children zipping up and down the stairs is unmistakable, the witnesses say.

Nobody knows exactly who these laughing, energetic spirits are, but at least they seem happy—just like the music that once filled Bennett House recording studios.

CHAPTER 12

RECORD SHOPS THAT ARE PARANORMAL HOT SPOTS

There was something magical about placing a round black chunk of vinyl on a turntable and suddenly hearing disembodied voices and heavenly ensembles of musical instruments fill the space around you. Records were like mystical, musical Ouija boards to perpetually connect you to your favorite artists.

Long before CDs and MP3s, iPods and Nanos, Spotify and Pandora became the listening medium of choice, crowds of country music fans shopped at record stores to buy black vinyl discs of their favorite songs.

Just as musical vibrations cause the impressions within the grooves of these records to permanently preserve the voices and talents of artists who may no longer be with us, paranormal researchers say that the spiritual energy of the departed can etch their impressions into the very fiber of our reality. If we're lucky—or unlucky—enough, or if we are just particularly receptive to these vibrations, we may be able to witness the manifestation of people who etched their spirit grooves into the very environment that surrounds us.

As we have read so far, ghost hunters tell us that spirits have carved their energy into some of Nashville's most famous landmarks. Some of those landmarks just happen to be, aptly enough, record stores. We'll tour two of the most famous haunted record stores in Nashville now.

ERNEST TUBB RECORD SHOP

Ernest Tubb was one of country music's most beloved stars and his eponymous record store soon became a favorite hangout for music lovers in a city populated largely by music lovers. As time went on, though, these music connoisseurs began to notice that not all the vibrations in the shop were caused by the stereo system.

The shop, located on Broadway, is one of Nashville's most notoriously haunted hot spots. Current and former employees are among the most knowledgeable sources on the supernatural occurrences and they believe the property is veritably spinning with spirits. If the employees aren't having run-ins with ghosts, they are fielding reports from customers who have had their own spooky encounters.

Witnesses have claimed they have suddenly felt rapid changes in temperature. The space around them would become unexpectedly hot or unexpectedly cold—a classic sign of a ghostly presence. Other people felt someone touch them, only to turn around and discover that they are completely alone. Still others say that, despite being in a good mood, they were completely taken up in feelings of grief as they shopped or worked at the record store. Then, just as suddenly, the grief seemed to dissipate.

The supernatural activity can reveal itself in other forms. Sometimes, for example, the CD player took requests, even when there was no DJ around to man the device. Customers holding conversations with fellow customers or a friendly employee will mention the name of an artist. Without warning, the CD player spontaneously begins playing a song by that very artist. It has happened so many times that it goes beyond coincidence or Jungian synchronicity, staff members say.

A few experts on the case pinpoint the basement and the staircase that leads to the basement as hot spots for the record store's haunting. The heightened activity in those spots appears to be related to the building's Civil War history. Long before it became a record store, the building was used as a hospital during the ferocious battles that raged around and in the city of Nashville. The basement, which is cool and dark, local historians point out, may have been used as a morgue. It's no wonder, then, that spirits seem to be more attached to those areas of the property because they are quite likely the last place their mortal selves inhabited, according to these experts.

LAWRENCE RECORD SHOP

One of the oldest record shops in Nashville doesn't just share the same stretch of street as two of the city's most famous haunted locations—Tootsie's and the Ernest Tubb Record Shop—but it shares some of its Civil War past with those places, as well. Historians believe Lawrence Record Shop, just like Ernest Tubb's shop, was once used as a hospital.

But the casualties of war are only one potential cause of the supernatural goings-on that are reported in the building. Most people theorize that it's the spirit of a former owner that's stirring up all the weird activity. The owner, known for his cigar-smoking, makes his presence known in an odd way.

Customers will complain to employees that they smell cigar smoke. Since smoking is not allowed in the building, staff members used to investigate. I said "used to" for a reason: while employees once rushed to the site where witnesses claim they smelled the cigar smoke hoping they could catch the scofflaw stogie-handed, they aren't in such a rush anymore. Typically, when employees investigated, they didn't find a cigar smoker. In fact, they couldn't find anyone near the scene—or maybe the smell—of the crime. These haunted snipe hunts happened so frequently that workers just nod to the complaining customer and say that it's probably Mr. Lawrence, as they call him, the long-dead owner of the record shop.

Other phenomena include mysterious light flickers and odd knocking sounds, the sources of which no repairman can seem to find. Witnesses also hear noises that they can only describe as footsteps marching up and down the steps leading to the shop's upper floors. When they look to see who is coming up the stairs, no one ever arrives.

Paranormal researchers say that more than one ghost can inhabit a space and Lawrence Record Shop may be a perfect example of this. As we discussed in the section on the Ernest Tubb Record Shop, the neighborhood that surrounds the record shops was near the scene of brutal fighting during the Civil War and many of the buildings in the area were used as hospitals for the Battle of Nashville, as well as other battles that consumed Tennessee during those violent months and years. In fact, according to several historical sources, the building where Lawrence Record Shop is now based was a hospital. The treatment that the men received there was primitive—and painful. There were no advanced types of anesthesia, or highly effective painkillers, as there are now. Often, the pain in the hospital was worse than the pain on the battlefield.

According to the researchers, this type of trauma creates the conditions for hauntings. It may be that, in addition to the record store's owner, ghosts of Civil War soldiers continue to tromp up and down the steps of the building.

CHAPTER 13

FREAKY FREQUENCIES:
GHOSTS OF COUNTRY RADIO STATIONS

Country music needed rural listeners and rural listeners needed radio. It wasn't like they could just head into the big city to catch their favorite artists. Radio and radio shows—like the *Louisiana Hayride* and the *Grand Ole Opry*—brought country music to them.

As country music grew to be a dominating force in entertainment—competing on the musical front with jazz and big band and later rock and roll—radio stations became powerhouses of country music, powerful enough to turn local or regional singers into national celebrities.

There are several paranormal theorists who suggest that radio stations didn't just power careers, they could power supernatural activity. The people who believe that radio stations are exceptionally haunted have two questions: Does it have something to do with the powerful transmitters booming out wave after wave of electromagnetic waves? Or does the psychic power of music become embedded in the atmosphere of these high-spirited spaces?

I'll let you consider those theories as you read about the eerie airwaves of country music radio.

KMCM RADIO STATION: TUNING IN TO SPOOKS

Back in the 1970s, most country music fans tuned in to KMCM, a radio station in McMinnville, Oregon, for their daily fill of country tunes and ballads. The station even said that the "MCM" part of their call letters stood for "More Country Music."

The formats and owners may have changed many times over the years—and even the call letters have changed (the station became KLYC in 1990). But one thing has remained: the radio station's haunted legacy, a legacy documented by a former news director at the station.

Tim King, who collected, wrote, and delivered the news for KLYC back in the early 1990s, told the *Salem News* that his experience working at the radio station is one reason for his interest in ghost hunting. He said that part of his duties at the station was to increase the AM's power for the day as soon as he arrived for his morning shift. For anyone who has ever picked up a Chicago radio station while on vacation in North Carolina, AM signals tend to go haywire at night and most AM stations alter their power during the nighttime hours and return them to full power at the start of the broadcast day.

The equipment to power up the station was located in what employees referred to as the rack room, a narrow space in front of the studio where the DJ worked. King would enter the rack room and flip a few switches to start the "warming up" phase to prepare the station to go live. The warm-up phase took about fifteen minutes, and during that time the employee was usually on edge.

He called it a feeling that was as inexplicable as it was uncomfortable. The feeling—or whatever it was that flooded the DJ during the process—was often coupled with a chill. Oregon winters might account for some of that coldness, King told the *Salem News*, "but there were sometimes more goosebumps than usual."

King continued: "I felt like I was sharing space with someone and neither of us liked the other very much."

Sometimes, though, it was more than just a feeling. He often would see something—an image, a figure—dashing by his peripheral vision. He turned to look at whatever was racing by. But it would be gone. It's easy to dismiss this as either imagination or perhaps the powerful radio equipment in a confined space was producing an electromagnetic effect that the radio station employee was picking up. But King said he knew there was something there. He didn't fear it; in fact, he became more and more interested in discovering the source of these phenomena. King and his wife had several discussions about the ghostly occurrences that seemed to be happening at the radio station.

When Halloween approached, King searched for a supernatural angle to spice up his newscasts. He began to research some of the local hauntings and sought out local paranormal experts. That's how he got connected to a local clairvoyant. The clairvoyant was quoted in a story about a haunting at Pacific University. When King contacted her, he told the clairvoyant that he was experiencing some weird stuff at the radio station. She agreed to come to the station on the day before Halloween for an interview—and perhaps an investigation.

Before the psychic arrived, King popped by the program director's office to brief him on the special Halloween show. As the program director listened, he interrupted his news director.

"Well you know this place is haunted, right?" The program director asked rhetorically. "You know there's something here, you open the station in the morning, don't you?"

King had never told the program director what he experienced, so this was a complete shock to him. He only talked about the haunting with his wife. The program director continued his story, telling the now completely stunned news director that every worker who ever opened up the radio station in the morning had reported encounters with the supernatural of one form or another. There wasn't a single employee who opened up the station who wasn't a little spooked by the place, the program director continued.

This was quite a bombshell to go off right before the interview with the psychic. When the psychic arrived, she toured the station and immediately picked up on a vibration, or a presence. The vibe was particularly strong in the rack room where King had his own run-ins with the phantom, she told them. However, the psychic felt that the power from the transmitter seemed to be blocking her. The psychic's impressions backed up his own experiences and their interview was a big hit among the listeners.

"I found it all very fascinating and it was good to know that I wasn't imagining the strange presence each early morning," he said.

King eventually left the station but, years later, found himself back in McMinnville. He visited his old workplace, which was no longer a radio station; it was now a daycare center for disabled children. He asked one of the women working at the center if she or any other employee experienced haunted activity. Her answer "made my skin crawl," he said.

The employee told King she needed some supplies, so she walked into a storage closet. After she opened the door, a tape dispenser flew in front of her. It wasn't like it tumbled off the shelf, either. There was no one there and the dispenser flew at such a high speed, the employee ruled out anything accidental or natural. Someone—or something—with a pretty strong arm tossed the tape at her, she said.

King now was a little better versed in paranormal phenomena. He wondered if the tape-tossing spirit was actually a poltergeist, a type of spirit that most paranormal investigators are familiar with. They are known for mischievous activities, like throwing objects and causing electromagnetic disturbances. Poltergeists are also noisemakers. In fact, *poltergeist* is a German word for "noisy spirit."

However, a poltergeist is often attached to a person, typically an adolescent or young adult. So, it didn't exactly fit the modus operandi of the spirit that King encountered. To this day, King looks back at that odd time at the radio station as a defining moment in his life—one that led him to exploring other signs of the supernatural. He investigated ghosts in nearby Pacific University and at cemeteries in Yamhill County. But those are only a few of the ghost hunts the former radio station news director has attended. He's investigated "dozens" of cases and has come to the conclusion that there are things that exist that seem to defy what the rational mind defines as real and natural.

"And yes, I have seen some things that go far beyond reasonable explanation," he told the paper.

But he'll always wonder: what made that radio station so haunted?

FRESH COUNTRY 103.1:
A TALL TALE OR A TALLAHASSEE TERROR?

The traffic reporter for a Tallahassee television station and morning DJ for the area's country music radio station reports he had an unscheduled cohost in the studio with him on a few occasions. The DJ, who goes by the name Big Moose, provides country music and news for his audience each morning on Fresh Country 103.1 in Tallahassee. Big Moose now believes that the studio is haunted.

One time, when he was alone in the studio preparing to give the traffic report for the television station, he heard voices and then heard—very distinctly—the voice of a little girl say, "Can you hear me?" There was no one around and it didn't seem to be any bleed through from any other studios or broadcast. The voice was that plain.

"Can you hear me?" The voice said again. Over the next few days, the voice called out again and again—usually at the same time.

Other activities baffled the DJ. He said doors would open and close by themselves. The staff, likewise, complained the computers would turn on and off without any explanation. Besides these anecdotes, evidence was hard to come by, though. There are dozens of natural explanations that skeptics could level at these supposed paranormal reports. For example, vibrations can cause doors to move and computers are notoriously temperamental, turning on and off with a will of their own. But then the staff at the radio station claimed to capture video evidence of the spirit.

One employee noticed something strange when Big Moose was giving his televised traffic report—an orb zipped around the room. Other people agreed. They saw it, too. There was some type of odd object swirling around the studio. If it was natural phenomena, it was really uncommon. No one ever noticed this type of effect on television before, at least.

Usually, when you encounter this weird behavior, you'll discover a ghostly legend about the building and, sure enough, Big Moose said he found a possible connection between a tragic event and the haunting activity he was experiencing at the station. According to Moose, many years before owners built the studio at its present location, the building was just a residential home. The family that lived in the home included a brother and sister. The bedroom for the children was located in the same place as the studio where Moose seemed to be experiencing most of the haunted activity—although, to be sure, the whole site seemed possessed by unexplained forces. According to the story that Moose retold, the children were playing, jumping up and down on the beds, as kids do. The brother jumped into the sister, knocking her toward the window, which was open. She went out head first through the open window and plummeted to her death.

Now the questions begin: Is this the girl that Moose hears? Is her spirit the one that was caught on video flitting around the studio?

Moose—and a whole lot of other believers—seem to think so.

CHAPTER 14

HAUNTED COUNTRY HOTELS

Some country music artists and fans get a two-for-one special when they stay the night at inns, hotels, and motels with a haunted reputation. They can hang out with fellow guests—and ghosts.

In our next section, we will explore some of those hotels with a paranormal past. These aren't just haunted hotels, though. The hotels that we will visit have a connection with country music. Some of the hotels are spots where country musicians perform and stay. There are a few places that may not have any country celebrities but are haunted by country music fans. Still others are located in the heart of the country and western music industry.

Our first story, for example, takes place in the Ozarks, not too far away from Branson, Missouri, what's been described as a little Nashville. And just like its big sister city in Tennessee, Branson has a lot of spirits and spooks.

BIG CEDAR LODGE: BIG SPIRITS IN BIG CEDAR LODGE

People travel to Big Cedar Lodge, a resort about ten minutes from Branson, to get away from it all, as long as when they say "all," they aren't referring to ghosts.

The lodge is located in a paranormal nexus in the Branson area and serves as the setting for some of the region's most famous ghost tales. It is a region, you have to remember, that was, at one time, one of the remotest sections of the Ozarks. Before the Great Depression, this area became a getaway for some of the more successful business people in the area, people like Harry Worman, a railroad tycoon, and Julian Simmons, an entrepreneur. These two neighbors in Springfield, Missouri, bought some land in this little stretch of wilderness paradise for their own vacation homes.

Inviting friends and family to the Big Cedar, Worman and Simmons entertained and enjoyed the wildlife and beauty of the Ozarks. As darkness consumed the wilderness and eventually surrounded their lodges and as roaring bonfires began to crackle and sizzle, the masters of the lodges must have told their guests about the ghosts that still haunted the woods of Big Cedar. It was well-known. The first settlers of the region—groups of American Indians—believed the ground was haunted.

A spring-fed pool that eventually became known as Devil's Pool was a bottomless pit, which, some say, led right to the depths of hell. One of the legends concerning this spot is that spirits of Native Americans haunt the pond.

Another legend in particular kept settlers on edge. The tale starts with a young man who was coming back from a date with a girl who lived near his home. The date must have gone alright because the man realized time had slipped by so quickly that he never noticed how completely dark the forest had become, with only a few silver rays of the rising moon to light his path back home. His path home, unfortunately, would go right past the haunted Devil's Pool.

While he was walking near the pool, he heard a groan. It sounded like some massive vault was opening. He couldn't believe his eyes. The once mirror-smooth surface of the pond started to bubble and boil. From the four corners of the forest, clouds of buzzards emerged and began to circle around Devil's Pool.

The man remained completely still, hidden in the brush. As the moon continued to rise, the buzzards suddenly took off and began to prowl the night sky. He said he watched some return and swoop toward the water. A splash would echo, like the birds were dropping something into the pond. Over and over, the bizarre ritual continued until, as dawn neared, the same groaning noise erupted in the dim light and the buzzards began to fly away.

The man hid the whole night! He survived, however. When he greeted relieved friends and family, they told him stories that all had not been well that night. They were experiencing their own bizarre phenomena, just not as up-close and personal as the man's front row seat for the occult. Area residents reported that during the night a wave of paranormal activity was unleashed. Some said that pets were afraid to go outside and stood at the open door barking at the night and warning their owners not to venture out. Birds clawed and tapped at windows throughout the night. Other people said they saw wild animals in masses and packs.

So, what was going on that night—and other nights when strangely similar activity has been reported? Some people claimed that the devil himself was sending the animals out to fetch him human souls.

The Swimsuit Satanist

Worman and Simmons shrugged off the legends and tales of soul-eating devil birds. They built their vacation cottages on that haunted stretch of the Ozarks—something that they may have regretted later, especially Worman, who brought his young wife to his vacation home. His wife, Dorothy, stood out in the small rural community. First, she was about half Worman's age. That raised some eyebrows.

The way she dressed really raised eyebrows. Or, rather, the way she didn't dress raised eyebrows. She went to the post office in a nearby town once while wearing nothing but her swimsuit—something that proper ladies just did not do back then—or even now, for that matter.

Then, there was her odd fascination with Devil's Pool. People said they saw Dorothy at the pool at very odd hours and she—allegedly—liked to visit the pond at midnight. Well, it doesn't take a genius to understand what these rumors actually meant: Dorothy was visiting the pond because she was cavorting with demons and spirits.

Showing up at the post office half-naked is one thing; swimming with demons, that's an entirely different category.

Another rumor spread that she had an affair with a member of the staff and fled with her lover to Mexico. She came back, though. But just as suddenly as she reappeared, she disappeared. This time it was permanent. The wife died and tongues nearly wagged out of their mouths. Everyone believed that foul play was the only explanation for a wayward young wife to die before her rich, but much older, husband.

Soon after her death, a story that a ghost walked among the woods and quaint cottages began to circulate around the area. In fact, dozens of people have reported seeing a woman walking through the grounds. It's quite a vision: a woman with long brown hair and a flowing white dress, a dress that doesn't quite seem like anything in the current fashion. Then there's her expression. The face of the woman seems so unbelievably sad.

Just a guest unhappy with her stay? Hardly.

The dress and the expression aren't the only things that seem unusual about the woman of the woods—she appears almost see-through. And she doesn't really walk as much as she glides.

Most of the witnesses believe that they have seen the ghost of Dorothy. Others go one better: they have evidence. Several guests who have taken pictures find odd images in their photographs. They look a little more closely and believe they can see a woman in the shot, even though there was nobody in, or even near, the spot when they snapped the picture. Those in the know say it's Dorothy.

Not all the phenomena is visual. People hear strange noises—and even voices—that they attribute to Dorothy. Others report a soft touch on their shoulder, like someone is tapping them, or touching them to get their attention, but, when these folks turn around, there is no one there.

WALKING HORSE HOTEL: THE HAUNTING OF ROOM 203

Although the Walking Horse Hotel is located just outside of country music's haunted capital, when it comes to country music and ghost stories, this hotel can compete with some of Nashville's biggest, brightest, and spookiest venues. In fact, it might just top them on a ghost-per-square-foot basis.

Paranormal investigators have just recently gathered evidence at the Walking Horse Hotel and their conclusion: the hotel isn't just haunted, it's one of the most haunted places in the country. These investigators have collected dozens of electronic voice phenomena (EVP) samples, including voices talking and singing, which may not be too strange because the Walking Horse is also a popular music venue.

The new owner of the hotel—Joe Peters Sr.—allegedly found out about the supernatural nature of his recent acquisition within days of taking over the establishment. The accounts of the paranormal and unexplained began to trickle in to the newbie hotel owner. Most of the tales would be filed under classic paranormal phenomena: strange noises, creaks and groans, and doors that seem to close by themselves.

While Joe said he personally believed in spirits, he didn't totally buy these stories. After all, the majestic brick beauty he bought was old and had lots of history—those factors are usually enough for guests to believe every creak and every flickering light is caused by ghostly intervention. He chose to discount the stories.

But the new owners could only ignore things for so long. As they started a restoration effort on the ground level of the hotel, the paranormal phenomena began to flare. (The paranormal aficionados would note that rehabilitation on old buildings tends to kick up more than dust out of the structures; it can kick up spirits, too.) While they worked on the building the owner and his family stayed overnight in the hotel. He could hear noises, but he didn't recognize the source. Again, the owner just thought his mind was playing tricks on him. It was the best excuse.

Later, he stayed overnight in Room 203. The noise of a train woke him up and he did what most people do when they have a little insomnia—he turned on the television set and tried to find something decent to watch. At 2 a.m. it's not an easy thing to do. Since there was nothing on, he turned the television off and lay back down, hoping the insomnia had finally lifted. But as he did, he felt a definite touch on his chest. At first, he didn't know what to make of it. He tried to sit up, but couldn't. It was like a tremendous pressure was on his chest. Now, most people would go into panic mode, but this hotel owner knew exactly what to do. Relax. Isn't that what you're supposed to do in a nice hotel? Once he completely let go, the spirit—or whatever you want to call it—let go, too, and he could move.

The spirit really knew how to announce its presence. Even the next morning, the owner was sore from the experience and decided to reach out to a psychic. The psychic had some interesting—and chilling—news. She said that the home was haunted and that a group of ghost hunters had conducted an investigation without the owner's knowledge. During the investigation, the paranormal investigators tried to provoke the ghosts. In some paranormal circles, that is a real no-no.

Joe's son said they had several—not just one—experiences with a ghost in the Walking Horse Hotel. In one case, the son was walking down the darkened hall, near room 202, not too far from where his father had his own encounter. Joe Jr. said he was walking by the room when he saw a figure and then heard a sharp hiss. Initially shocked, he quickly regained his composure, figuring that his dad was probably behind the stunt.

You can guess what happened next. He eventually found his father far away from where he encountered the hissing spirit. There was just no way his dad could have surprised him and made it back to that room in time.

The spirits weren't quite done with the father and son. The elder Peters was walking out of the laundry room and heard a guttural growl. The sound seemed to be right next to him! Keeping his cool, he just kept walking and said, "Get lost," to the growling ghost. He sensed that the spirit didn't really listen and followed him into the hotel's music hall, where most of the concerts are staged. That's when Joe Sr. had another idea: maybe the spirit was as afraid of loud noises as he was. He was about to give the ghost a taste of his own loud medicine. He sat down at the drum set and began to pound away.

At the same time that Joe was getting into a drum-off with a ghost in the music hall, his son was sitting with his girlfriend on the couch. They had their own story. As they watched television, their miniature schnauzer startled awake and began to look into the kitchen. But there was nobody there. The dog began to growl and the hair on its back stood straight up. There was something in the kitchen that was freaking out the pooch, but the couple could not figure out what.

When Joe Sr. came in and told them his story, they pieced together the mystery. Apparently, the dog began to behave strangely mere moments after the drum solo scared off the ghost from the music hall. They guessed the ghost was chased right up to the apartment, where the dog must have sensed its presence.

Not all the apparitions are blurry or visible only to acute canine senses. Staff members report they have had direct contact with—and even spoken with—full-bodied apparitions. One worker said during Halloween the hotel gets into the festivities, decorating each room with a different theme. He was in one of those theme rooms when a small girl walked into the room and said her name was Emily. Emily then proceeded to pull up a chair next to the surprised worker and recanted an odd tale—an odd tale for such a young girl. She said she died in the hotel after a fall.

The employee was surprised because Emily didn't fit the description of anyone staying in the hotel. She wasn't the daughter or relative of any of the staff members, either.

In fact, the little girl who sat next to the worker fit the description of another hotel spirit. Since the 1970s, people have reported seeing the ghost of a young girl in the hotel. Those reports continue to come in. What's perplexing about this entry on the hotel's long list of ghostly sightings is there doesn't seem to be any confirmation of the spirit's story that she fell to her death. This has led to another theory about the haunting, but we'll get to that a little later.

Believe or Else

The spirits that haunt the hotel apparently aren't satisfied with spooking guests or surprising members of the hotel staff. They want *you* to believe. A few skeptics have stepped forward and said they received physical reminders that spirits were nearby and they wanted to convince them of their reality.

One person said he was physically attacked by an unseen presence. The witness—or victim, depending on how you want to view the incident—weighed about 250 pounds, not someone who could be pushed around easily. He admitted that earlier that evening he made some disparaging remarks about people who believed in ghosts. He added he would have to be convinced.

He got his wish.

Later that night, he was standing in the third-floor corridor when something struck him. The blow sent him reeling. The force pushed him, nearly lifting him off of his feet, he said. Let's just say he has no problem believing in ghosts now.

The man's brother got a little supernatural warning, too. He was chatting with three paranormal investigators on the paranormally active third floor on Halloween night. Without any seeming provocation, the man was struck hard in the stomach. The blow bent him over.

Later, he recalled making a few snarky remarks about requiring proof to believe in ghosts. Like his bro, he got confirmation and to this day, he believes the Walking Horse is haunted and that ghosts exist.

Calling in the Investigators

As the volume of paranormal encounter reports at the Walking Horse began to amass in staggering numbers, the owners decided it was time to turn to the experts. They called in groups of paranormal investigators and some of these teams say they collected evidence that a real haunting was underway in the establishment.

A member of one of those groups seemed to have an unusually good rapport with the spirits of the Walking Horse Hotel. She was able to consistently gather clear EVPs while investigating there. In one case, the investigator was talking to one of the owners during a session. However, the session was interrupted when the investigator was called downstairs. She went back upstairs to complete the EVP session and began to ask questions again. Unable to find the co-owner she had originally been working with, she asked—out loud—if he was still in the room. Later, when the team analyzed the audio file, they heard a voice say, "He left the room!" in response to the investigator's question.

This same investigator had another wild incident during another session. After one particularly grueling investigation in the hotel, she was standing on the side porch as other team members were packing up their vehicles, calling it a night. They heard the unmistakable sound of a horse whinnying and running in a nearby field, about thirty yards from the property. Some of the investigators also said they heard the clip-clop of horse hooves hitting the asphalt. The trouble was … there were no horses nearby. Out of nowhere, a breeze kicked up and the leaves rustled around. What was particularly odd for these researchers was that the morning had been devoid of wind. It has been totally still before—and after—this event.

Another paranormal group reports that they divided into teams—one would explore the dining rooms and the music hall, another took on the third floor. The team on the third floor entered one room and seemed to stumble on a conversation between a man and a woman. Though they listened intently, they couldn't make out the actual details of the conversation. Some of the equipment that the team carried to pick up electromagnetic signals started to go haywire. As the tempo of the paranormal activity cranked up, a team member saw a shadow slither across the floor in his direction and then disappear.

At the same time, the other team was experiencing similar phenomena. They saw a shadow creature and heard voices at the exact same time. Once they re-formed, members of both teams went to the third floor, yet again, for one more attempt. When they were in the hall, they heard noises coming from a room. They went into the room. As they entered the room, they heard the same noises, except they were now coming from the hall. They went out in the hall, the sounds were emanating from in the room again. The investigators believed that the spirit was toying with them.

Perplexed, the team split up once again. One group covered the room, while the other waited in the hall, hoping they would hear the voices. Instead, they claimed that they heard a "very strange laughter."

It looks like, according to this wily spirit, the joke was on them.

Full-Bodied Apparition

As the ghost hunters' account of the joking ghost seems to indicate, the spirit—or spirits—that haunt the Walking Horse do not want to be seen. They like to toy with their victims. But at least one decided to show itself.

According to two investigators, a full-bodied apparition appeared to them as they were exploring the third floor. They were initially drawn in by the sounds of—very faint—voices and whispers that echoed all around them. A loud sigh further grabbed their attention. But that was nothing, relatively.

Suddenly, a long shadow appeared in front of them. It was so large that it completely blotted out the door. As the investigators stared at the shape, one researcher saw a woman—attired in a dress and fashion from a much earlier age. Even though the witness was no stranger to the weird world of paranormal researching, he nearly flew out of his skin, jumping two feet into the air and dropping his flashlight. He struggled to get his colleague's attention to see the ghostly woman; according to the account, he "nearly tore his shirt off trying to grab him to show him the woman." The vision finally disappeared.

According to the latest reports, the spirit may have disappeared, but the haunting at the Walking Horse Hotel continues, as does the good music and great times.

THE STOCKYARDS HOTEL: OUTLAWS AND OUTLAW COUNTRY ADD UP TO OUTRAGEOUS HAUNTINGS

When country music stars are in the Dallas–Fort Worth area, they like to stay at the Stockyards Hotel. The hotel's Celebrity Suite, for example, has been the room of choice for country and western music legends including Tanya Tucker, Trisha Yearwood, and the King of Outlaw Country himself, Willie Nelson.

It's not just outlaw country musicians who stay in the Stockyards Hotel. Actual outlaws Bonnie and Clyde found the hotel, located just a couple miles from downtown Fort Worth, a nice place to get away, in all senses of that term.

But country stars and bank robbers aren't the only frequent visitors at the Stockyards Hotel. Some guests just keep coming back again and again.

And again.

The Stockyards Hotel, a favorite of both country stars and country fans alike, is haunted. Built in the epicenter of Fort Worth's world-famous cattle market, called the Stockyards, the hotel was built specifically for rich cattle barons and livestock traders who would spend a lot of time—and loads of money—in the Wild West town.

Experts on the supernatural phenomena at the hotel say several spots in the hotel seem to be more haunted than others. The elevator, for example, has a mind of its own. It will go up and down without anyone clicking the buttons. It's been repaired numerous times over the year, but the odd activity continues.

It's not just a mechanical haunting, though. Some people have been riding the elevator when a little girl gets in. She looks like any other little girl, but people note that her clothing seems from another era, maybe from the 1920s, they guess. The girl doesn't say a word, she turns to face the elevator door and when it opens on the second floor, she takes three steps out of the door—and disappears.

Spooky Quake

A recent visitor, who was staying on the second floor of the hotel, wrote about her own strange experience in an online review. Although she and her sister, who were standing near the famously haunted elevator, didn't see the ghost of the little girl, they felt a strange disturbance—almost like the earth was moving beneath them. She said that she became dizzy and then it felt like an earthquake had hit Fort Worth. Her sister also felt the quake and was equally disoriented. More troubling, people passed by the two ladies, seemingly unaffected by the tremors that were enveloping them. It was almost like the two were caught up in some field of energy, she writes.

Eventually, the guests made it out of the hotel and sucked in some fresh air. According to the desk clerk there were no earthquakes in the area, nor was the building undergoing any unexpected shifts from construction projects. However, later, some employees reached out to the women, confidentially, and told them that the spirit of an elevator operator still haunts the place.

It was the employees' bet that the ladies experienced some type of psychic reaction to this spirit.

In an online review, the two women seem to say they might come back to the Stockyards Hotel, but they probably won't stay on the second floor. They'll probably take the stairs, too.

Room 218 gets a lot of the press for being haunted. Guests there say they have experienced the whole spectrum of paranormal activity—from hearing voices to seeing objects move. Dozens of ghost hunters—and just people who want to have the bejeezers scared out of themselves—have made that room a focus of their investigations.

The entire second floor, by the way, seems like a hot spot for ghostly activity. Female guests also complain to staff that while they are sleeping, they feel like someone crawled in bed with them. When I say "complain," that's not quite the word. They usually ask hotel workers to find them another room. Immediately.

Employees and former employees of the Stockyards Hotel have lots of their own ghost stories. One desk clerk said that a telephone call came in. The employee answered it. As soon as he said hello, the caller hung up. It happened again. And again. Finally, the employee noticed that the call was coming from a phone in the lobby. The phone rang again. This time he decided to lean forward so that he could see the lobby and the joker who was making the prank call. The joke, however, was on him. He could plainly see the phone was hung on the wall, exactly as it was supposed to be. To this day, the worker is convinced that the phantom caller was just that, a phantom who was alerting him to his ghostly presence.

Bonnie and Clyde Suite

Lots of people request the Bonnie and Clyde Suite, the room, legend has it, that the infamous couple stayed in while they were on the lam in Fort Worth back in 1933. The room is full of actual artifacts from the outlaws reign of terror, including reportedly Bonnie's .38 revolver, photographs, and newspaper clippings. A poem that Bonnie Parker wrote for Clyde Barrow is also prominently displayed.

But there are other mementos from their stay—including the restless spirits of the gangsters themselves. People have reported a range of anomalous activity that indicate they are continuing their stay at the Stockyards Hotel, from electromagnetic disturbances to a water faucet that turns on and off by itself.

Night Life and Death in Fort Worth

According to a lot of the paranormal buffs—people who actually seek out ghosts and spirits—the great thing about staying at the Stockyards Hotel, besides the great country music that is part of the fabric of Fort Worth nightlife, is that the hotel is surrounded by other haunted buildings. The Stockyards is both haunted and historic.

Everything that a fan of country music—and the supernatural—could want.

MAISON DE VILLE: BIGGER COUNTRY FAN IN THE BIG EASY

You might not expect to find country music fans in the swanky Hotel Maison de Ville—which is French for "townhouse" by the way—and its cottages hanging around the cosmopolitan heart of the French Quarter. After all, New Orleans is a jazz city.

But you would be wrong.

There's at least one permanent guest of the Maison de Ville who loves his country music and you better not touch his radio. This guy isn't going to call hotel security on you—but he may just haunt you for the rest of your stay. This ghost of a country music fan is allegedly just one of the spirits roaming this property. For example, according to guests and staff at the hotel, there is definitely a spirit in one of the former slave quarters that now serves as suites for hotel guests. But there could be more.

According to most reports, the ghost of a soldier appeared to a hotel employee in a suite usually identified as Cottage 9 a little more than two decades ago. The staff member, who worked at the hotel for twenty-seven years, said the ghost was unmistakably a soldier; he was wearing a sharp military uniform, possibly from World War II. Shocked, the employee said she felt a chill and shook involuntarily as she remained eye-to-eye with this vision. The ghost, then, just disappeared.

Most people think the ex-soldier's ghost is behind some of the other haunted high jinks in the hotel, too. For instance, many workers have said that as they are cleaning or repairing the suite the radio comes on. And it's country music that is blaring at top volume. Of course, the workers turn it off. They leave the cottage and go about their daily routine. As they exit, they notice that music is playing—and they eventually realize the tune is coming from the suite that they are sure should be vacant. When they retrace their steps and open the door to the cottage, country music is again blaring from the radio.

On other occasions, workers and guests made the mistake of switching the radio to another station. Big mistake. The radio is immediately switched back to his favorite station, the one playing country music. In fact, one employee said she intentionally switched the stations back to a boring old classical music station on several occasions. Each time, the radio went back to kicking out that good old country music.

So, who is the man behind the ghost?

It's hard to say. The hotel—and especially the former slave quarters—have witnessed their share of tragedy and their share of powerful personalities, both can prompt hauntings. The hotel has a long history that makes it difficult to isolate one cause of the haunting. After all, the hotel includes structures that are among the oldest standing buildings in New Orleans. Some of the city's most colorful characters lived or stayed there, too.

Antoine Amédée Peychaud, a druggist who had a business in the building, took bitters and brands and mixed up one of the Big Easy's most famous drinks called Sazerac. He might have gone from making spirits to becoming a spirit, according to some experts on New Orleans hauntings.

While we don't know whether Tennessee Williams was a country music fan, he did stay at the Maison de Ville in Room 9. The playwright reportedly finished *A Streetcar Named Desire*, one of his most famous works, while living there. When he took a break, Williams often sauntered into the courtyard and enjoyed a drink. Some say the writer's ghost still inhabits the property.

You might recognize the name John James Audubon. He was the naturalist and artist who is most famous for his paintings of birds. Audubon was a guest at the Hotel Maison de Ville and, in fact, he worked on his famous Birds of America series at the hotel. The Audubon Cottage is named for the artist.

So, with this list of spirit suspects, the hotel may be located in the Big Easy, but it's not that easy to find the source of all the supernatural activity at the Maison de Ville.

SECTION 3

MISCELLANEOUS HAUNTED COUNTRY PLACES

In our next section, we will take a look at haunted places that don't easily fit into the previous categories, so they are mysterious but also miscellaneous. Some of the following ghost stories are connected to country music's most famous celebrities. I thought, for example, you might want to discover a ghost or two lurking in Elvis Presley's hometown of Tupelo, Mississippi. I also wanted to pass on a few tales about outlaw country ghosts. Not all the stars in country got their start singing in church. A few singers began their careers in the gut of the most depressing—and possibly haunted—prisons and reform schools in America, places like Preston School of Industry and Folsom State Prison.

But it's not just buildings that can be haunted and it's not just people who can be spirits, according to many paranormal theorists. Supernatural events can cover vast swaths of land, they say. It's as if the land itself is imbued with occult power. Some of those haunted hot spots are located in the South and Midwest, the heart of country music.

Certainly, one could make the accusation that the entire city of Nashville is haunted. With its violent Civil War history mixing with the high spirits of country's biggest dreamers, Nashville has more ghosts on a per-block basis than other cities. But, as mentioned before, Branson, Missouri, a popular new site for country music, is situated in the center of one of America's most mystical regions—the Ozarks. While maybe not as densely populated with spooks as Nashville, it runs a pretty close second when you consider the ghost stories that surround the second city of country music.

Interestingly, these haunted regions don't just become the stuff of legend in country music; they become the stuff of songs. Much of the ghostlore in these places became fodder for country songwriters. We'll review a couple of those tunes and trace back their narratives to country music's most haunted places.

CHAPTER 15

OZARK SPOOK LIGHTS:
BRANSON'S BIG LIGHTS

Branson, Missouri, is a little like a Phoenix.

No, not the city in Arizona.

The little city in the Ozarks has been through a lot. Like a lot of towns in the South, Branson earned its scars during the Civil War. The city also endured a horrible fire that scorched much of its historic downtown area about a century ago. The city, however, went from battlefield to playground and from the ashes of that horrible fire to a city of lights, crowds, celebrities, and music—and a lot of that music is country music. Despite the flash and excitement, Branson still shows the scars of its past in unexpected, unexplained ways, particularly in the form of ghost stories and haunted legends.

Branson and the Ozarks, as we will read, are inundated by stories of ghosts and spirits.

Celebrities who have turned the town into the new Nashville, lovers of great country music, as well as ghost hunters return from their trips to Branson with stories that suggest ghosts inhabit many of this musical city's most famous locales.

Lee Prosser, author of *Branson Hauntings*, writes that while you're visiting Branson to see your favorite country acts, you can also find some haunted locales to investigate. And it won't be hard—Prosser said that the Ozark Mountains is a center for supernatural activity.

The roads in and out of Branson—the same ones that country and western acts have traveled for decades—are haunted, as are the railroad lines and the streams that roll off the picturesque foothills.

Some tourists head to the Branson Scenic Railway for a real train ride through the Ozarks. It's a way of touching the past and viewing the rough and beautiful terrain of the Ozarks as visitors did decades ago. There's another piece of the past they may encounter during their visit: ghosts. According to Prosser, the railroad's depot is built near the super-haunted White River and is, in fact, the subject of several ghost stories. Witnesses have reported seeing the ghosts of a couple walking near the depot. While a romantic stroll around the depot isn't unheard of, these witnesses say that the couple is peculiarly dressed in 1930s-era clothing. The ghost of a young boy has also been spotted in the vicinity.

There's something else that spooks people about the Ozarks. In fact, it's probably why everyone calls the bizarre lights that pop up in the region, "spook lights." One of the most famous examples of these alleged spook lights is just a short distance—about a two-hour drive—from Branson. It's so well known in Branson, because, depending on which way you're headed into the town, your path may go directly through the haunted region known for this anomalous activity.

People in this area—and people who travel along the long stretches of road from Missouri to Oklahoma—claim to see large glowing orbs above the road. Sometimes, they float down the highway, like lost souls looking for a ride home. Other times they head right for the car. There's at least one cabbie who claimed the spook light went right through his taxi!

If you're a brave soul on your way to Branson and want to catch a spook light, your best bet, experts say, is to head down County Road E50, better known as Spook Light Road. The lights there demonstrate a range of behavior. Some witnesses have reported seeing the light appear—usually about the size of a basketball—and dance around in a more or less random pattern. But other sightings indicate that the light has some sort of awareness, maybe even curiosity. The light will appear and then float around. If the vehicle is parked, the light may even wander up to the hood of the car. It's almost like the spook light is trying to see who is in the car, according to amused—or horrified—witnesses.

Several of those witnesses have gone on record in Mysterious Universe, a website that tracks bizarre Fortean occurrences and supernatural phenomena. Roberta Williams, a resident of Carthage, Missouri, said she was taking a late-night drive when she saw a spook light. And she's no longer a skeptic. She believes it was a real thing.

"It was before midnight," she said. "It was like a big, huge ball with a yellow glow and it went right straight through our car. I just screamed."

Skeptics say there are natural explanations for the light show. Some say it's ball lightning—a type of electromagnetic phenomena that's similar to regular lightning, but tends to stay compressed and not spread out in bolts, the shape lightning commonly takes. Some say it's gas escaping from the swamps and from the shale formations. Others say that it's the lights from car headlights that is refracted in the moist Missouri air. A few believe that the lights are UFO's—after all they do fly, they are objects, and no one can identify them.

Several researchers and groups of engineers have scoured the back roads and explored the forests in the area looking for an answer. They've pretty much come up empty. The US Army Corps of Engineers studied the area and never arrived at a satisfactory conclusion.

The ball lightning theory is difficult to prove because the phenomena is so rare that it makes little sense that a certain area in a certain state would produce it on a regular basis, researchers say, but nearby universities are still looking into the theory.

While scientists say they can't explain the lights, folklorists and ghost hunters have lots of theories. One of the most popular legends about the spook lights is an American Indian version of Romeo and Juliet. According to the legend, a young Indian man and woman were involved in a clandestine romance. They were in love, but they both came from warring groups. The woman's father found the two in an embrace and he—along with several other warriors—gave chase. The couple ran into the woods. They ran faster and faster, but the warriors and one angry father was right behind. The two never saw a cliff looming as they ran blindly through the thick brush. They fell off the cliff and died.

Legend has it that the spook lights you see are either the ghosts of the American Indian couple who still believe they are being chased, or, according to other versions of the legend, the lights are the spirits of the star-crossed lovers roaming the countryside, eternally lost, yet eternally looking for each other.

The persistence of the spook light legend tends to prove the veracity of the modern encounters. In fact, Seneca Indians who lived there reported seeing spooky orbs traveling around the countryside. So did early European settlers.

But another theory suggests that the spook lights have a much more modern and a much more otherworldly source. The lights are Unidentified Flying Objects—UFOs. The UFO theorists suggest that the crafts are using portals in the region as a way to traverse across the galaxies. This power portal theory may also explain why UFO sightings are more prevalent in other sections of the country, for example Roswell, New Mexico, the Hudson Valley, and Gulf Breeze, Florida.

The spook lights in Missouri, then, might just be another American UFO hot spot. But there's a key difference between this region and the other UFO hot spots mentioned above. Sightings in places, such as Gulf Breeze and the Hudson Valley, lasted a relatively short period. In the Ozarks, however, people have seen spook lights buzzing around for centuries.

So it looks like this one is still in the mystery category.

CHAPTER 16

BROWN MOUNTAIN LIGHTS:
SONGS PAY TRIBUTE TO THE MOUNTAIN'S WANDERING SPIRIT

We've read about the strange lights that soar and dash over the vast stretches of rugged roads in the Ozarks. In North Carolina, mysterious lights hover above the Brown Mountain. And just like the spook lights in the Ozarks, the North Carolina version of the phenomena has inspired fear and curiosity among the locals and songs among country and folk musicians.

No one knows when the lights first began to appear along the mile and half ridge that stretches along the Pisgah National Forest that meanders through North Carolina's Burke and Caldwell counties. Some say that Cherokee Indians were the first to spot the lights, possibly even as far back as the 1200s. But most of the documented cases start appearing in records during the nineteenth century.

Just to be clear, a lot of skeptics want to blame the lights on highway phenomena—swinging headlights for example—but these early cases were established well before automobiles were invented, or, at least, were common in the region.

Although the accounts are spread over hundreds of years, the descriptions of the phenomena are roughly the same. Often compared to a roman candle, the lights appear at the ridge top. They're extremely bright. Witnesses from dozens of miles away claimed to see the anomalous flames appear and then climb into the sky, before exploding and snuffing themselves out. Some of the silent explosions appear to climb well above the mountain. Weather is often to blame for the phenomena, but the lights appear irregularly, in all types of weather conditions and during all types of temperature variations.

Most people familiar with the Brown Mountain lights say you should view them from the Linville Falls, a scenic spot near the Blue Ridge Parkway.

That area has another bright spot—the musicians and songwriters who live there and fill the ridges and valleys in the area with country, folk, and bluegrass music. It doesn't take a genius to predict that good music and the spooky lights of the Brown Mountain would one day meet in song.

Scotty Wiseman was one of the first to talk about the strange lights near his hometown of Spruce Pine, North Carolina. Wiseman, now enshrined in the Nashville Songwriters Hall of Fame, and his better half, Myrtle Eleanor Cooper, formed the famous country and western singing duo, Lulu Belle and Scotty, often referred to as the Sweethearts of Country Music. One of the songs that Wiseman became most famous for was the tune "Brown Mountain Light." The lyrics of the song point to one of the spookier explanations for the light show.

According to Wiseman's song and other legends that have been passed around the hills and hollows of this section of North Carolina, the lights are from the spirit of a slave. The slave's master went hunting and got lost. He never returned to the plantation. His slave, though, went out to find him. As darkness was approaching, he made sure he grabbed a lantern and when he could see no more, he lit the lantern to continue his search. He never found the lost man, but he was so dedicated to that quest that he continued his search until he died. And even after his mortal body was laid to rest in the good North Carolina soil that he tromped on endlessly, his spirit continued his quest. The lights that people see on the mountain are from the lantern of this long-dead slave.

The song was covered by some of the most famous acts in country and folk music. The Kingston Trio and the Hillmen recorded versions.

Not everyone believes the story of the faithful servant spirit, but even scientists are forced to admit that something weird is happening on Brown Mountain. They're just not ready to label that activity supernatural—yet. Since the early twentieth century, researchers from the US Geological Society, as well as several groups of researchers from nearby universities, have investigated the lights. The researchers haven't convinced a lot of people with their theories, which blame everything from power lines to automobiles for the lights. Often these scientific attempts at debunking have been debunked by the Brown Mountain light faithful. For example, power to the power lines in the area was severed—once by flood damage—but the lights kept showing up. Car lights also seem like a convenient excuse for the researchers, but, as mentioned, some of the lights show up where there are no roads.

And that's where we still are today. Some people believe that the lights are supernatural, some people believe the lights are completely natural, albeit rare. The rest—like Roy Orbison and the Kingston Trio—are content to avoid the debate and just sing about the strange glowing orbs that haunt the hills of North Carolina at night.

CHAPTER 17

FIDDLER'S ROCK:
YOU HAVE TO HAVE A GHOSTLY FIDDLE PLAYER IN THE BAND

For most country music fans, it isn't country music unless the band has a fiddle player. The fiddle—which fans will tell you is just a violin played by someone who really means it—gives country songs that distinctive plaintive sound. Fiddle players, therefore, were given a place of honor in a country and western combo.

While you'll never get an argument from a fan that a fiddle is important to that country sound, you might get some raised eyebrows if you claim that fiddle players are magic. You won't get those strange looks, however, if you make that declaration in Johnson County, Tennessee, near a spot on Stone Mountain that most locals call "Screaming Rock." The haunted spot has a country music twist to it, though. Besides Screaming Rock, some residents refer to it as Fiddler's Rock. And there's a connection between the two.

If you visit the site on windy winter days, the legend goes, you can hear a high-pitched sound echoing through the trees. Now most of the unimaginative people you talk to will tell you it's just the wind whistling through the rock outcroppings. But there's another theory, one that is more supernatural—and far more fun.

The sound, they say, is actually a phantom fiddle player who is playing a haunting mountain melody. The story—a wonderful example of Appalachian ghostlore—goes on to reveal the name of the fiddle player, dubbed Martin Stone, who used the rock as an outdoor rehearsal hall. The fiddle player became a hot commodity, playing at dances and shows in the area as a featured performer.

People said Stone was a super fiddle player. You might say supernatural fiddle player. Mothers, for instance, who spent many sleepless nights trying to rock their teething babies to sleep would call Stone. It turns out, the moms didn't need to rock them to sleep—they needed to country and western them to sleep. When he would play, the babies would be soothed to sleep.

Stone's musical powers went beyond curing insomnia; he supposedly could also heal the sick. His most bizarre talent was not how he healed the sick, but how he soothed the beasts, particularly snakes. People said Martin could play so sweetly that rattlesnakes would crawl out from under rocks and stones and sun themselves as he played. Then he would shoot them with his shotgun.

One day, Martin's neighbors noticed that the sweet notes of the master's fiddle had stopped filtering down from the majestic heights of Stone Mountain—and there were no sounds of his shotgun, either. The neighbors decided to investigate. When they made it to the rocky outcropping, they found the lifeless body of Martin Stone. His body was covered in snake bites—and his hands were stretched out, inches away from his shotgun. He didn't make it to the gun in time.

Without Martin's soulful strings, the mountain was silent for a while. But then people began to hear the odd whistling from the mountain. At times, they could almost make out a tune. Most skeptics said it was either a practical joke or the winds were echoing through the stones. But others weren't so sure. They went to investigate when they heard Fiddler's Rock erupt in all its musical glory and they never found any pranksters. The music could be heard on windless days occasionally, too.

These believers had an explanation. The spirit of the aptly named Martin Stone—the magic fiddle player—was not leaving his beloved mountain, and he was never going to leave his beloved fiddle.

C H A P T E R 1 8

FOLSOM PRISON:
PRISONERS ETERNALLY
SINGING THE BLUES

We read about Johnny Cash and his haunts. The singer knew something about tragedy and how just a few tragic moments can echo across eternity. He wrote about it. He sang about. And some say he lived it.

One of Cash's most haunting songs is "Folsom Prison Blues," about an inmate who was forced to live the rest of his life with regret over his decision to commit a heinous act. According to stories that have trickled out of the infamous prison, the regret that some unlucky inmates have felt over their dark deeds during this life doesn't end in the prison morgue; their sentence of regret and anguish has turned from a life sentence into an afterlife sentence.

Guards and former inmates say that the facility is awash in phantom appearances and mysterious sounds; relics, they believe, of a long list of deaths that occurred there. Approximately ninety-three prisoners were executed at Folsom. That number doesn't include the ones that died of natural—and not-so natural—causes, nor does it include the guards who were murdered or died there.

One of the places where you'll hear stories of Folsom's paranormal side is at the prison museum. James Brown, a manager at the museum at the time, told the *Folsom Telegraph* that while he never saw a ghost there when he was a corrections officer—he's since retired—he believes in ghosts and has heard lots of stories about the ghosts that haunt Folsom.

"As a young man, I had a few experiences that convinced me (ghosts) exist," he told the newspaper. "I believe in them ... but I let them be and they leave me alone. Maybe that's why I never had experiences while I worked at the prison."

Brown said that because the prison is full of tragedy, it makes sense that the place is haunted, which is why he keeps looking for ghost stories.

"I've heard that places filled with tragedy and violence can be haunted," Brown said. "This is a prison—you have tragedy and violence in prisons. So, I asked about stories and listened."

One of the ghosts, according to Brown, is the spirit of a corrections officer who died when a prison riot broke out during a Thanksgiving meal. Prisoners didn't kill the guard—he died of a heart attack while under severe duress manning the front gate. Another guard, however, was stabbed to death in the melee. There is a debate as to who the ghost guard really is, but he's known simply as the Folsom phantom. (Some say that because the ghost is seen at the gate, it's the guard who had the heart attack—not the one who was stabbed—that can't seem to escape his prison watch.)

In either case, witnesses have seen him—usually on foggy nights—at the front gate of the prison, a shadowy figure that stands watch over the prison and walks slowly along the gate. Those who caught sight of the apparition say they immediately realize that he's not a guard, at least any sort of human guard. They say the ghostly guard has a human shape, but is almost see-through. More like a mist, than a man, they say.

Another infamous supernatural encounter occurred late one night. The story goes like this: in what had been an otherwise uneventful evening, the guards had settled into their normal routine, except for prison guards, there's no such thing as a normal routine. When things are exceptionally calm and quiet, that's when the guards get wary. That night, they had a reason to be anxious. The story that's been handed down over the years was that a couple of guards noticed a person walking down the corridor—and no one was supposed to be in that part of the prison. It must be an inmate, the guards immediately surmised.

They called out for the inmate to halt. But the figure disregarded the order and continued to walk down the corridor at a decent clip and vanished.

Fearing that a prisoner was escaping, the guards jumped into action. They gave chase to the figure walking down the hall and put the prison on high alert.

However, the man had just vanished. The guards sent to apprehend the escaping convict reported back that there was no trace of anyone down the long, dark, dank corridor.

And the tale gets weirder. Quickly, the guards ordered a headcount. After the headcount, the guards were mystified to discover that no one—not an inmate or a guard—was missing. Whoever was running down the corridor, it turns out, wasn't on any list of inmates or employees.

There are more tales of Folsom weirdness. While the whole prison appears to be haunted, certain spots are more active than others, according to Brown. The hospital is one of those primo places to witness the paranormal, he adds. Obviously, quite a few prisoners died in the hospital from natural causes. But it had a worse reputation. Brown said many of the murders that occurred in Folsom happened in the hospital. This may be one reason the hospital has become the institution's supernatural epicenter with dozens of apparitions and poltergeist-type activity being reported there.

Besides the hospital, ghosts also haunt the prison morgue. (Shocking, I know.) The row of jail cells that make up death row are allegedly haunted by the spirits of the prisoners that met their end by execution in the prison, too.

The prison, at least at this writing, is still in operation. It continues to be a place of punishment and—hopefully—reclamation for the lost souls who by either bad fate or bad decisions ended in the institution.

Oh, wait, did you think I was talking about the living inmates?

CHAPTER 19

PRESTON CASTLE:
THE REFORMATORY GHOST STORY

California, with its ample sunshine and radiant stars and starlets, may seem like a planet away from the "just folks" vibe of Nashville and other centers of country music culture. But a California town and its music style served as a cradle for several country acts that felt Nashville had become, ironically enough, too glitzy and out of touch.

That town is called Bakersfield. And it's every bit as hardscrabble and tough as the towns in the East that defined country music, like Nashville. Most, though, would say Bakersfield is tougher. The California town is also just as haunted as its Eastern sister cities—some might say more haunted.

The town teems with ghosts—and some are intrinsically connected to country music's most famous acts, including Merle Haggard. Haggard, along with other acts like Buck Owens, would go on to create that hard and haunted-sounding style of country music that is now called the Bakersfield sound.

One of Bakersfield's most famous—or infamous—landmarks is connected with country music and, specifically, with one of the architects of the Bakersfield sound. That musical architect, Merle Haggard, wrote songs about real music and real situations, all punctuated with the infectious, twangy hooks of a Fender Telecaster guitar. It wasn't the saccharinely polished ditties that Nashville record producers became so enamored with in the 1960s.

But Haggard didn't care. After all, he lived those real situations—and he wasn't afraid to talk about, write about, or sing about those hard times. In his rough and tumble youth, Haggard rode the rails and hitchhiked across the country. He even spent some time in San Quentin for robbery. But a tattoo Haggard etched on his left hand revealed what the songwriter considered the integral chapter in his life's story. The tattoo simply said *P.S.I.*

In Haggard's reckless youth, he committed enough minor offenses, such as shoplifting and theft, that he was placed in a number of juvenile detention centers, until he finally ended up in the Preston School of Industry—P.S.I. The school is housed in a formidable, castle-like building in Ione, California. Until 2011, it housed juvenile offenders and young wards of the state. While the center is no longer in operation, some of the wards of this impressive facility have not been released, nor have they been transferred.

The ghosts of Preston Castle, as the school is sometimes called, are still haunting the detention center, according to dozens of witnesses and ghost-hunting groups.

While he never mentioned it, Haggard may have heard a story about the leading suspect for the P.S.I. haunting—Anna Corbin. Anna was the head housekeeper at the institute. She was murdered and her body was discovered—some accounts report she was found in a storeroom—on February 24, 1950. According to police, she was bludgeoned to death, but the murder remains unsolved to this day.

Haggard arrived at the school a bit after the grisly murder.

Since the murder, Anna takes the rap for much of the paranormal activity that's reported in the reform school. And that rap sheet is quite lengthy. People say they've heard doors slam in the building; others claim that they haven't just heard doors slam, they have watched in awe as doors move on their own, then slam shut in one loud, echoing *bang*! To compound the mystery, the slamming door seems controlled, like someone is pushing it. It doesn't seem like the result of a draft or faulty door stop.

It's not just doors that move on their own. Witnesses have watched objects move along flat surfaces as if some force is pushing them, others have seen objects fly off shelves. Sometimes, people set an item down on a table or a shelf, look away, and when they look back it has disappeared totally.

It gets creepier. Staff members report hearing disembodied voices in the halls; others have heard a woman scream and, oddly, the sound of eggs frying in a skillet. (Hey, even ghosts deserve a good breakfast. It's the most important meal of the day.)

While, officially, no one has seen the ghost of Anna—or whoever the spirit is—people have claimed they were touched by a ghost, or say they felt a strange presence. There are even cases of a spirit possessing members of a paranormal research team investigating the haunting.

Ghost hunters have also offered photographic evidence— mainly pictures of orbs—as an attempt to prove that there are paranormal forces at work in the site of the former reform school. Recording devices have picked up some of the voices and the strange sounds mentioned above that researchers consider evidence of the haunting.

While Anna gets most of the attention—or blame—from spirit-seeking paranormal buffs, she's only one of the possible suspects for the school's alleged supernatural problems. The building has been the scene of lots of tragedies, including several deaths. According to some historians, dozens of students died due to sickness and disease. A guard reportedly shot an inmate during an escape attempt. Finally, some former inmates and former students have said beatings and other forms of abuse happened in the castle. The powerful emotions that are released due to the stress and strain could account for some of the paranormal activity that's been encountered at the site, according to paranormal theorists.

Did Haggard ever have an encounter with the supernatural at the reform school? If he did, he didn't seem to talk about it much. There's no mention in the records I've come across.

But it's interesting to consider that an influence on the famous Bakersfield sound was a lonely inmate serving not just a life sentence, but an afterlife one as well.

CHAPTER 20

WITCH DANCE
AND LYRIC THEATER:
ELVIS'S HOMETOWN HAUNTS

Tupelo, Mississippi, is known to country music fans as the birthplace of Elvis Presley. But long before being known as the birthplace of a superstar, it was known as the center for the supernatural.

Not too far from the city is an area called Witch Dance. A legend has been passed down from generation to generation that the forests in that section just south of town were haunted. Witches supposedly gathered in the woods and whipped themselves into a frenzy. They began to dance in a circle and as they did, they began to fly. Each time a witch touched the ground, she burned the grass. People familiar with this legend said that you can still find fresh patches of burnt ground that indicate witches still gather there for their nefarious midnight dances.

One doubter of the legend was Big Harpe, an outlaw who, along with his brothers, terrorized the region in the late 1700s.

An American Indian guide was leading Big Harpe through northeast Mississippi. Harpe was being chased through the wilderness around Witch Dance by a posse bent on revenge. Big Harpe noticed the strange burned grass patches and asked his guide about the odd markings. When the guide began to tell him about the witches sabbaths that were held in the section of the forest, Big Harpe just scoffed and began to dance himself, hopping from one burned patch to the next. He beseeched the forces to come meet him.

When nothing happened, he laughed even more, figuring that he just uncovered a hoax. But he may have spoken too soon. The witches didn't need to appear to the arrogant criminal to get even. Legend says they used their magical powers to allow the posse to find Big Harpe. The posse chopped off his head and nailed his skull to a tree. Now, people say, if you're quiet, you can hear Big Harpe's scoffing laugh echoing in the forest.

As Big Harpe found out, Tupelo is surrounded by terrain that can be at turns mystically serene and darkly disturbing. It's history is similar: the region can seem peaceful, but its legacy of violence and disaster is unavoidable. Battles with American Indians had no sooner ended than Confederate and Union armies were pitted against each other. It is said that those ghosts—the spirits of native warriors and Civil War soldiers—are still present in the small Mississippi city.

In addition to contending with man's inhumanity to man, the residents of Tupelo have also endured the power—and in some cases, brutality—of Mother Nature. In 1936, a tornado, estimated to be a monster F5 on the Fujita Scale, ripped through the city and destroyed homes, businesses, and houses of worship. In one macabre display of ruthlessness, the twister lifted a group of victims from the ground and deposited their lifeless bodies in a pond.

There were survivors. One of those who lived through the destruction was Elvis Presley, who was just an infant during the disaster. Another survivor was one of the town's most treasured paranormal properties—the Lyric Theater.

Elvis, no doubt, may have heard tales as he grew up about how the Lyric Theater, the town's main movie theater situated on Broadway Street, was used as a makeshift hospital during the aftermath of the tornado. Ingenious surgeons used the popcorn popping machine to sterilize their equipment, according to area historians.

Elvis, too, must have heard about the ghost—perhaps a ghost of one of the tornado's victims—that haunted the theater which some Elvisologists say became the scene of the King of Rock and Roll's first make-out session. Most folks refer to the ghost as Antoine. Legend has it that Antoine makes himself known through a series of pesky, mischievous, but not malevolent interactions. For instance, he likes to steal keys. Employees will flop a set of keys on a table or a counter for a few seconds and when they look back again, the keys are gone. Vanished into thin air. They usually turn up somewhere else in the theater, which only compounds the mystery.

The ghost also likes to hum. Customers and people who work at the theater say they hear a strange hum emanating from different spaces in the theater. People who have had the task of cleaning up the theater or doing repairs there late at night claim to hear spirit footsteps tromping around the building and have heard things dragging across the floor. Antoine, it seems, likes to remodel.

In Elvis's time, the theater was used almost exclusively as a movie theater, but it's now been renovated to include stages for theatrical presentations and concerts. It plays a key part in Tupelo's various Elvis celebrations, too.

While legends about Antoine have been circulating around Tupelo for decades, the renovations have apparently increased the number of run-ins with the spirit. One community theater volunteer said that the legend is not fiction; he has returned to the theater early in the morning after a rehearsal or production only to find "everything moved."

The volunteer, along with dozens of other Lyric Theater believers, think that, unlike Elvis, Antoine has not left the building.

CHAPTER 21

HAUNTED JUKEBOXES:
JUST PRESS B-SCARED

The spirits of the dead find ways to communicate with the living. They are not above trying out some weird ways to make that contact, either. According to paranormal researchers and spirit mediums, these messages can come through Ouija boards, the movement of objects, and the sudden presence of intense feelings and emotions. Sometimes, they'll just show up and have a conversation.

Other times, they'll just play you a song.

At several bars, clubs, roadhouses, honky-tonks, and restaurants, there are reports of jukeboxes operating autonomously. They'll play songs inexplicably, when no one selected the song. Sometimes the jukebox isn't even plugged in when it belts out a tune. In more extreme examples, these jukeboxes not only fire up unexpectedly, but they play tunes that are no longer on the machine.

We'll start this exploration of paranormal jukeboxes with a visit to a familiar stop on our way through haunted country music: Bobby Mackey's Music World.

BOBBY MACKEY'S AND THE ANNIVERSARY WALTZ MYSTERY: WILDER, KENTUCKY

As we discussed earlier in the book, Bobby Mackey's Music World in Kentucky is one of the hottest—and most haunted—country music destinations. According to witnesses and experts on the haunting, a focal point of the honky-tonk's haunted history seems to be the old jukebox in the ballroom.

Several witnesses—including ones who actually signed affidavits to their testimonies—said that they saw and heard the jukebox turn on spontaneously. In one case, two witnesses heard "The Anniversary Waltz," a song published in the 1940s, crank up. When they cautiously walk toward the jukebox to investigate, the instant they step into the ballroom the song stops.

A police officer responding to a burglary alarm at the honky-tonk—false alarms happen with an almost preternatural frequency at the bar—said that as he entered the premises the jukebox was on, playing tunes from the 1930s and '40s. Other witnesses corroborated these reports, saying that they, too, have heard 1930s-era music echoing from the building and also assumed it was the jukebox cranking out the old school tunes.

Even weirder, during several instances, the jukebox played even though it was either unplugged or the power was off in the building.

A manager of the bar has the best story. She stated that the jukebox started to play when she entered the building. Not only was it not plugged in, but the spindle was not revolving, there was no record on the spindle, and the song that was playing was not on the jukebox's playlist!

One man said that the haunted jukebox even haunted his dreams. During a night of paranormal terror, he dreamed he heard a gunshot ring out. The echo of the shot was still reverberating when he heard the jukebox kick on and play "The Anniversary Waltz." There's no real information on why the song is connected with the haunting, which may involve several spirits, including the ghost of a murder victim.

Gathering Spot for the Supernatural

The jukebox at Bobby Mackey's Music World seems to be a center for the haunting there in another way—it seems to attract ghosts. Several people have seen apparitions near or by the jukebox. One person said an apparition walked right by the jukebox, another saw an apparition standing near the machine. The obvious speculation is that these ghosts are the ones requesting the songs.

In another horrifying example of Bobby Mackey's haunted jukebox, at least one club regular paid the paranormal price for standing close to the machine. A man said he watched in terror as a filmy white apparition drifted across the club toward the jukebox. At the time, a band member was standing next to it. The ghost approached the man and then, apparently, slid right into his body!

Filmy ghosts, ghosts on two legs, ghosts with no head, and at least one of their four-legged ghost friends seem to congregate around the jukebox. According to one story in *Hell's Gate*, a book written about the haunting, a woman saw a huge black dog running behind the club's stage. Then she heard someone shout her name. The instant she turned around to find the source of the shout, the jukebox began to blare. No one else was in the club at the time, let alone close to the jukebox.

COUNTRY HOUSE: CLARENDON HILLS, ILLINOIS

While the jukebox played favorite songs of the 1950s, a young lady and her small daughter entered the establishment that most locals call the Country House, according to the legend. The pretty blonde woman cut like a knife through the dining room toward the smooth bartender pouring drinks at the bar. She was obviously on a mission. The bartender and the blonde had words.

While the legend of this haunting has few details on the conflict between the woman and the bartender, there is speculation that the two were involved in a romantic relationship—and that relationship was about to split irrevocably. Good love gone bad? That sounds like a good plot for more than a few of those tunes playing on the jukebox.

In any event, the words turned into an argument and the argument drew the attention of the tavern's customers and staff. Feeling the public attention, the woman became embarrassed and spun around to exit the bar. She swept her little girl along with her, like a twig caught in a strong river current.

The story turns tragic. Just up the road from the tavern, the woman's car reportedly careened off the highway and into the tree. Some say that both the woman and the daughter died; other sources suggest only the woman died in the accident, but most people believe that the tale did not end completely that horrific evening. They say that the spirit of this fate-crossed lover lives on—and the jukebox plays on.

Since the night of the accident, restaurant staff and patrons report that the jukebox is restless, playing songs when nobody has deposited any money. In some cases, the songs echo long after everyone has gone home and only a few stray employees are left cleaning up and preparing to close.

In one of the more frightening encounters, a worker was toiling away on a project to renovate the tavern. He took a bathroom break and just as he exited the bathroom, he says he heard music playing. The worker knew he did not play any tunes. He proceeded directly to the bar area. There, swaying in the dim light of the jukebox, was the figure of a gorgeous blonde woman, dancing under the spell of the music. Maybe the worker figured this woman slipped in from the street or that she somehow never left after last call, but he walked toward her to confront her and ask her to leave.

That's when he got the shock of his life—as he looked down, the worker noticed that the woman was invisible from the waist down.

The jukebox isn't the only thing that's haunted in the restaurant. A wide range of paranormal happenings have occurred on the premises. The blinds open and close on their own. Pots and pans rattle. Sometimes, according to the legend, guys say they are drawn to the restaurant because they see a pretty blonde woman in the tavern window. She seems to be motioning them to join her.

Who could resist, right?

But when the men walk into the tavern, after desperately checking every stool and booth, every chair and table, they can't seem to find her. They then ask the bartender where the hot blonde went.

The bartender smiles knowingly to himself, looks over at the seemingly empty spot by the jukebox, and wonders whether they really want to know.

LOCALS BAR AND RESTAURANT: PAWNEE, ILLINOIS

What is it about Illinois and haunted jukeboxes?

Another bar in Illinois—Locals Bar and Restaurant—is also reportedly outfitted with a haunted jukebox.

According to one newscast, the bar has experienced some haunting activity for years. The activity was so intense that a group of ghost hunters were called in and said their investigations revealed at least two ghosts were stalking the premises.

At least some of the paranormal outbreaks center around the jukebox. If you know anything about bar culture, you'll realize that jukeboxes help create the bar's atmosphere. It's a pleasant environment when everyone likes the song that is playing, but these music machines can turn that harmony into discord if someone plays an unpopular tune. Probably the biggest debate in the war on jukebox aesthetics is between country music fans and rock music fans. That seems to be one of the ongoing paranormal debates in Locals Bar and Restaurant, too.

According to one worker, the bar's jukebox—which turns on by itself at odd hours of the morning—has a mind of its own. It also is played by ghosts with an eclectic range of musical interests, and, quite possibly, at least one country-loving ghost.

"It's a very random genre—I've heard 'Girls, Girls, Girls' [by metal band Mötley Crüe] and then country," one worker told a reporter from WCIA, an Illinois television station. "So, one is a rock fan and one likes country, apparently."

The workers are stumped why the jukebox sounds at 3 a.m. In order for it to play, someone has to physically input the dollar and make a selection. It's not as if the jukebox can be accessed online, for example.

In addition to the ghostly jukebox, people claim to hear footsteps and door knobs twisting. At least one person encountered an apparition walking down the stairs.

EARNESTINE & HAZEL'S: MEMPHIS, TENNESSEE

You can't walk by the buildings of downtown Memphis, Tennessee, the home of the blues and the old stomping grounds of Elvis Presley, without wishing for those walls to somehow talk. Patrons, workers, and ghost hunters say that at least in one of the city's bars, you don't need the walls to talk, the jukebox is chatty enough.

Earnestine & Hazel's is one of Memphis's most storied bars. It's also one of the city's most "ghost storied" bars. Some experts on the haunting suggest that the—well, let's call it—"unique" history of the operation is the reason for its ultra-haunted reputation. Over the years, a number of businesses were centered there, including an upstairs brothel.

According to several stories that have grown up around Earnestine & Hazel's, not all the women who were employed at the brothel were happy about their situation in life. In fact, some were despondent. In one tale, a prostitute committed suicide in a second-floor bathroom. She continues to haunt the establishment. Some people who are walking near the area where she took her own life say they are inexplicably struck with a feeling of intense sadness. They were perfectly happy just seconds ago.

But it's not just feelings that warn patrons of a spiritual presence—they say if you listen closely you can hear the ghosts. The bar's jukebox turns on spontaneously—just like a few of the other haunted music machines we reviewed. However, the spirits may embed messages in the lyrics and song titles of the tunes they select. For instance, Michael Einspanjer, a Memphis-based paranormal researcher, asked for any ghosts on the premises to reveal themselves at the end of his investigation. The jukebox kicked on and began to play a song with the lyrics, "Can you see me? Can you see the real me?"

Spooky, for sure, but at least this haunted jukebox also seems to have a sense of humor.

WHY ARE JUKEBOXES HAUNTED?

There are a lot of theories as to why jukeboxes are so haunted. Some paranormal theorists suggest that, as we mentioned, these music-makers help spirits communicate with fellow bar and restaurant patrons. Spirits use the device to say they are there and possibly add clues to why they remain attached to the establishment.

Another completely different school of thought proposes that the jukeboxes, themselves, are haunted. This theory is usually referred to as the haunted objects theory—or cursed objects theory, depending on the outcomes of the haunting. According to this idea, just as a house can be haunted, so can an ordinary object. In paranormal lore, there are haunted dolls, haunted chairs, and even haunted paintings. You can even buy some of these haunted objects on eBay. Why you would want to do that, I can't even guess, but the opportunity is definitely there.

Similar to haunted objects, cursed objects appear to be haunted, but their presence creates negative situations for people who touch, handle, or own the object.

Finally, people in the paranormal community often debate whether a spirit is possessing these objects, or, oddly enough, the object has its own spirit. The advocates of this theory say that the jukebox itself is a spirit, which adds a whole new level of creepiness to this phenomenon.

Whether it's a ghost by the machine, a ghost in the machine, or just a ghostly machine, we can conclude that haunted jukeboxes are—and will be—integral to country music and country music ghostlore.

CHAPTER 22

HAUNTED TOUR BUS:
WHISPERIN' BILL ANDERSON RIDES WITH THE MOANIN' GHOST

Tour buses are houses on wheels for country music veterans who use the mobile mansions to perform for fans all over the country. Sometimes, they can be haunted houses on wheels.

Whisperin' Bill Anderson was a veteran of country music tours. He has been performing for more than fifty years and his performances and songwriting—he's won several awards for both—were enough to propel him into the Country Music Hall of Fame. A 2010 tour of Canada, however, propelled the singer into the Country Music Haunted Hall of Fame.

Anderson and his band claimed that an unexpected guest climbed aboard their tour bus for a twelve-day trip through the country. By the end of the tour, the group was convinced their tour bus was haunted.

The signs that a paranormal traveler had hopped on their bus began as soon as they embarked on the tour, the hall of famer said. Anderson, as well as his band and crew, heard a moaning noise. The moaning seemed to emanate from the bus's state room, located in the back of the bus. Despite several attempts, they couldn't find a rational explanation for it.

But the supernatural tour was just beginning.

Later, the crew heard a scream that was so audible and clear that, believing that a real emergency had taken place, the driver pulled the bus to the side of the road. They were worried they hit someone. The driver checked and found nothing. They also discounted some type of mechanical problem that might cause the squeal.

After that check, the crew realized nothing was wrong—nobody was in pain; nobody seemed to be hurt. The tour mates chalked up the incident to the bus's ghostly passenger. (Later, Anderson speculated that there may be a few ghostly passengers responsible for the haunting.)

The crew even videotaped the aftermath of the haunted happenings, showing a few very concerned tour mates, along with, what sounds like, a faint, but high-pitched scream.

The investigation into the paranormal seems—by all indications—to have stopped at the end of the tour. The reasons behind the haunted tour bus remained a mystery. There's no suggestion that, for example, the bus was involved in a fatal accident. Anderson, though, wondered whether some of his old buddies might be pulling a practical joke on him, except that these old buddies were long-dead friends and country music soul brothers, Hank Williams and Faron Young, the country singer best known for his rendition of "Hello Walls."

"I'm trying to figure out if it's Hank Williams wanting to cow-rite a song or Faron Young just messing with my head," he told country music journalists.

EPILOGUE

MUSICAL SPIRITS
AND THE ULTIMATE QUESTION

This is my third official—as in, contracted and published—book that delves into ghosts and ghostlore. When I talk to the media and chat with readers, they generally have two questions in common. I'll save the second one for a little later, because we'll want to deal with the big question first. Ultimately, people want to know one thing: Is this stuff real?

I can tell you—after these three books and a hell of a lot of research, dozens of interviews with skeptics and believers alike, and hours dwelling on this stuff in the early morning—that this question has become harder, not easier, for me to answer. The supernatural is more layered than the binary—believer, skeptic—way of thinking about it that is portrayed in the media.

As a person who enjoys reading folklore and mythology, I recognize that there are elements of these ghost stories that reso-nate with certain mythical themes and reflect common motifs of folklore. Often the real reason we tell scary stories, pass on urban legends, and study other forms of folklore rests beneath the mere facts or the clever narrative of the tale. Folklore often carries important messages—life lessons and warnings, for example—and preserves them in the culture's collective consciousness.

We have reviewed many examples of ghost stories-as-mythology in this volume of country music ghostlore. For example, Hank Williams's ghost, who haunts just about every stop he and his young chauffeur made during his infamous last ride in that baby blue Cadillac back in 1953, not only helps us recount the last breaths, last steps, and last words of one of the country's most pioneering superstars, but can also stand as a cautionary tale, warning us all about the high cost of fame and fortune.

Ghostlore may exist for another reason. In a fragile and transient world, these tales serve as a repository to forever preserve the memory of our favorite artists and celebrities.

This is how many skeptics—at least the more polite ones—respond to questions about ghost stories featuring Elvis, Hank, Patsy, and the rest of country's pantheon of paranormal stars. Joe Nickell, a senior researcher for the Committee for Skeptical Inquiry, for example, writes in *The Skeptical Inquirer* that the ghostlore of Elvis and tales of the King faking his death are nothing but a mythical extension of the Elvis impersonation industry.

He writes: "The impulse that prompts Elvis encounters is the emotional unwillingness of fans to accept his death. This is the same impulse that has helped fuel the Elvis-impersonator industry, just as it made possible the impostors of an earlier time who claimed to be the 'real' death-surviving cult personalities of John Wilkes Booth, Jesse James, or Billy the Kid."

In addition to the cultural motivations behind telling ghost stories, skeptics can come up with a range of natural explanations—including deception, hallucination, misidentified natural phenomena, etc.—for encounters, too.

But if we immediately dismiss all ghost stories as overzealous fan worship, mythological obituaries, or fraud without analyzing the facts of each story, we are not skeptics at all; we are cynics. Complete cynics are more like total believers than they care to admit. They are just total believers in the opposite direction.

As a journalist and research writer, I'm trained to avoid taking evidence of the supernatural—or evidence of any experience, for that matter—by faith alone. Journalists are conditioned to simply present the details, as best they can find them, and leave the speculations to the readers. In fact, some—certainly not all—of the accounts I have written about pass key tests of journalistic credibility. These stories detail how honest, thoughtful people have encountered events and phenomena that they could not attribute to natural phenomena. They have witnessed objects moving by themselves, heard the sounds of voices when nobody is present, and even saw the appearance of ghostly figures. Often, several witnesses encounter the same activity at different times but relay nearly the same account. More perplexing, some stories include groups of witnesses who experience the same phenomena at the same time. Any journalist will tell you that corroborating witnesses lend credence to the story.

But it's not just the accounts that I have included in these books that make me wonder if there isn't an anomalous basis for at least some of these ghost stories. As I give talks or go to book signings, I have met dozens of people who tell me personal stories about encounters with ghosts, spirits, and other paranormal phenomena. Some of these tales are related to the stories in my books, some are not. These folks, on the whole, seem smart and well-balanced, and, while I don't know their entire psychological history, they don't seem to be people who are prone to hallucinations. Certainly, they don't seem prone to hallucinations at a specific time or place. Generally speaking, someone who is delusional doesn't just see visions, or hear voices when they are in the Ryman Auditorium, or on a tour of Graceland, and be psychologically healthy the rest of their life, for example.

Some of these accounts have come from unexpected sources, too.

On more than one occasion I've chatted with some of the most hardcore, nonbelieving materialists and realists, who, in a comfortable setting, will drop their guard and tell stories that unveil gaps in their own rigid assessments of the paranormal. In one case, a scientist, who had only a few hours before joined in mutual derision of UFO kooks and Woowoo flakes (I think he called them) with his colleagues, began to tell a story that could only be described as a ghost story. He said shortly after his mother died, objects began to fall off shelves and glasses began to shatter—spontaneously. The weird events only ceased after the intervention of a family member.

Apparently, his estranged brother, who did not show up at the funeral, returned to make peace with his departed mother and the crashing and smashing quit. In a phrase that any Woowoo flake would have appreciated, he said that it was almost like peace had returned to the home. A few other scientifically-minded types joined in with their own stories, too, among bursts of nervous laughter.

Just like the scores of believers who have shared their accounts with me, these skeptics considered their own experiences with the unknown and bizarre to have deep, spiritual meaning, even if they refuse to allow these events to interfere with their day jobs.

So, let's get to the second question. The other question I'm typically asked is: Do I believe in ghosts?

I still maintain my open-minded skepticism, which means I haven't been completely convinced either way. Even the best witness testimonies of ghosts and spirits can have holes. But so do the scientific explanations that try to explain away anomalous phenomena. I'm also reminded that science is often caught off guard by the discovery of strange phenomena that doesn't quite fit current paradigms. Einstein's theory of relativity, black holes, quantum mechanics, and string theory all were once fringe ideas held by an extreme minority of the scientific population. Paranormal theorists, I might add, have almost as much physical evidence for the existence of ghosts as string theorists have for their own ideas on how the universe works.

To convolute my answer even more, it may turn out that the either/or thinking of both the scientists and the paranormal researchers are misguided. Stories of encounters with ghosts and other mysterious forces, along with scientific theories of quantum cats and vibrating subatomic strings, may point to a deeper truth: that our reality—the one we live, sleep, love, play, and work in—is just the tip of a much vaster smear of infinite possibilities.

NOTES AND RESOURCES

HANK WILLIAMS

Hank Williams's Death Ride is detailed in several different accounts. The ride I use in this book relies primarily on Hank Williams fan sites.

Resources:

Bullock, Mark. "Alabama's Ghost Hunters." 12 WSFA. http://www.wsfa.com/story/7294214/alabamas-ghost-hunters

CMT: "Spirits of Country Music," http://www.cmt.com/news /country-music/1458426/the-spirits-of-country-music.jhtml

Ellison, Curtis. *Country Music Culture: From Hard Times to Heaven.* Jackson, MS: University Press of Mississippi, 1995.

Ghosts of America: "Oak Hill," http://www.ghostsofamerica .com/2/West_Virginia_Oak_Hill_ghost_sightings.html

Gina Lanier: "Haunted Cemetery Ghost," http://ginalanier.com /CEMETERYGHOST.php

Hank Williams: "Last Ride," http://hankwilliams.nl/english /death/ride.html

Haunted Jaunts: "Ryman," http://www.hauntjaunts.net /tennessee-spirits-the-ghosts-of-the-volunteer-state/

Koon, George William. *Hank Williams, so lonesome.* Jackson, MS: University Press of Mississippi, 1983.

Marsh, Donna, Jeff Morris, and Garett Merk. *Haunted Nashville Handbook (America's Haunted Road Trip).* Cincinnati, OH: Clerisy Press, 2011.

Mystery441: "Old Covington County Jail", http://www.mystery411.com/Landing_oldcovingtoncountyjail.html

JOHNNY CASH

Cash, Johnny. *Cash: The Autobiography.* New York: HarperCollins, 2003.

Go Nomad: "Annie Palmer: The White Witch of Jamaica," http://www.gonomad.com/1103-annie-palmer-the-white-witch-of-jamaica

Mysterious Destinations Magazine: "Close Encounters at the Johnny Cash House," http://mysteriousdestinationsmagazine.com/close-encounters-at-the-johnny-cash-house

Nashville Music Guide: "Growing Up Kilgore, the Johnny Horton Story," http://www.nashvillemusicguide.com/growing-up-kilgore-the-johnny-horton-story/

Rose Hall: "Cinnamon Hill Great House Tour," https://www.rosehall.com/tours/rose-hall-great-house-day-tour

Turner, Steve. *The Man Called CASH.* New York: Thomas Nelson, 2005.

Upvenue: "7 Interesting Facts About Johnny Cash," http://www.upvenue.com/article/1471-7-interesting-facts-about-johnny-cash.html

This YouTube video contains an extensive interview with Merle Kilgore on a few of the incidents discussed in the paranormal partnership of Kilgore, Johnny Cash, and Johnny Horton. https://www.youtube.com/watch?v=mmEtBlGTPjE

ROY ACUFF

Biography.com: "Roy Acuff," http://www.biography.com/people/roy-acuff-20641565?page=2

Country Rebel: "Top 5 Most Haunted Places in Nashville," http://countryrebel.com/blogs/videos/74350403-top-5-most-haunted-places-in-nashville

Marsh, Donna, Jeff Morris, and Garett Merk. *Haunted Nashville Handbook (America's Haunted Road Trip).* Cincinnati, OH: Clerisy Press, 2011.

Nashville Real Estate Blogger, http://nashvillerealestateblogger.com/?m=200810

PATSY CLINE

American Hauntings: "When Stars Fall from the Sky," http://troytaylorbooks.blogspot.com/2013/03/when-stars-fall-from-sky.html

Bastion, Lam. *The Airplane Crash that Killed Patsy Cline.* Amazon Digital Services, Inc., 2011.

Ghosts of the Prairie: "Ghosts of Ryman Auditorium," http://www.prairieghosts.com/ryman.html

Ghost Village message board, Ghost of Patsy Cline, http://www.ghostvillage.com/ghostcommunity/index.php?showtopic=25161

Hazen, Cindy, and Mike Freeman. *Love Always, Patsy*. New York: The Berkley Publishing Group, 1999.

York Daily Record: "Yorker Haunted by Patsy Cline," Archived here: http://web.archive.org/web/20150716020704/http:// www.ydr.com/mike/ci_25684647/mike-argento-yorker -haunted-by-patsy-cline

Patsy Cline fan site on Facebook page includes a brief history of the home and historic pictures here: https://www.facebook .com/media/set/?set=a.553740041318937.137046 .135670573125888&type=3

LORETTA LYNN

Country Music Highway: "Every Museum Has A Story," http:// www.countrymusichighway.com/EveryMuseumHasAStory .html

Ghosts of the Prairie: "The Haunting of Hurricane Mills, Home of Loretta Lynn," http://www.prairieghosts.com/hur_mills .html

Lynn, Loretta, and George Vecsey. *Loretta Lynn: Coal Miner's Daughter*. New York: Vintage, 2010.

Taste of Country: "Loretta Lynn's Plantation House to Be Featured on Travel Channel's 'Ghost Adventures' on June 10," http://tasteofcountry.com/loretta-lynn-ghost-adventures -june-10/

Theresa's Haunted History of the Tri-State, http://theres ashauntedhistoryofthetri-state.blogspot.com/2013/04 /kentuckys-van-lear-coal-miners-museum.html

Van Lear Historical Society, http://www.vanlearkentucky.com
/ghost.html

ELVIS PRESLEY

Alastar Packer, http://alastarpacker.weebly.com/mists
--moonlight/alastar-packer-haunted-graceland-and-a
-ghostly-encounter-in-memphis

Dixie Spirits Blog: "Elvis Lives! Spectral Sightings of the King of
Rock n Roll," https://ckc4me.wordpress.com/2013/05/16
/elvis-lives-spectral-sightings-of-the-king-of-rock-n-roll/

"The Ghost of Elvis Presley," http://crazyhorsesghost.hubpages
.com/hub/The-Ghost-Of-Elvis-Presley

Ghosts of Graceland: Archive X, https://web.archive
.org/web/20051030081430/http://www.wirenot.net/X
/Articles/2005/G/ghostsofgraceland.shtml

Many examples of Elvis's ghost, including several videos
on YouTube, including this one: Elvis Presley's Ghost at
Graceland on 11-23-14 !!! must see, https://www.youtube
.com/watch?v=9v53nlAXgBU

MINDY MCCREADY

E Online, http://www.eonline.com/news/382780/mindy-
mccready-denies-she-killed-boyfriend-david-wilson-blasts
-reports-of-an-affair

Perez Hilton, http://perezhilton.com/2013-02-22-mindy
-mccready-dead-boyfriend-visited-her-before-her-suicide
#.Vjs8v7erSM9

BERNARD RICKS

The Chimes, December 1961 http://www.ehbritten.org/docs
/chimes_december_1961.pdf

Turner, Steve. *The Man Called CASH*. New York: Thomas Nelson, 2005.

THE RYMAN AUDITORIUM

Ghosts of Tennessee: "Ryman Auditorium," http://tn_ghost
.tripod.com/sites/reports/ryman_auditorium.html

Ghosts of the Prairie: "Ryman Auditorium," http://www
.prairieghosts.com/ryman.html

Haunted Places to Go: "Haunted Places in Tennessee—the
Ryman Auditorium," http://www.haunted-places-to-go.com
/haunted-places-in-tennessee.html

Hoobler, James A. *A Guide to Historic Nashville, Tennessee.*
Charleston, SC: The History Press, 2008.

Ryman Auditorium website, http://ryman.com/history
/captain-tom-ryman

OPRYLAND

Appalachian Ghostwalks: "Tennessee Ghosts and Haunted
Places," http://www.appalachianghostwalks.com/tennessee
-ghost-stories-haunted-places/nashville-ghosts.html

Coleman, Christopher K. *Ghosts and Haunts of Tennessee*. Winston-Salem, NC: John F. Blair, 2011.

Fun Times Guide: "Looking for Ghosts & Haunted Places in Tennessee," http://franklin.thefuntimesguide.com/2006/09/tennesseeghosts.php

Ghost Place message board: "Opryland Hauntings," http://www.ghostplace.com/threads/opryland-hotel-hauntings.6511/

Ghost Stories and Haunted Places: "Black Lady of Opryland," http://ghoststoriesandhauntedplaces.blogspot.com/2011/04/black-lady-of-opryland.html

Haunted Places: "Gaylord Opryland Resort," http://www.hauntedplaces.org/item/gaylord-opryland-resort/

THE MUSIC CITY CENTER

Unexplainable: "Haunted and Scary in Missouri Part 3," http://www.unexplainable.net/ghost-paranormal/what_s_haunted_and_scary_in_missouri_part_3.php

APOLLO CIVIC THEATRE

The Herald-Mail, http://articles.herald-mail.com/2002-01-28/news/25122646_1_ghost-stories-ghost-hunters-paranormal-activity

Huntingdon Paranormal: "Haunted West Viginia," http://web.archive.org/web/20160113215106/http://www.huntingtonparanormal.com/hauntedwv.html

SHREVEPORT MUNICIPAL AUDITORIUM

20 X 49 Shreveport-Bossier website: "Is This a Ghost at Shreveport Municipal," http://20x49.shreveport-bossier.org/index .php/2012/08/02/is-this-a-ghost-at-shreveport-municipal -auditorium/

Joiner, Gary D., and Cheryl H. White. *Historic Haunts of Shreveport.* Charleston, SC: The History Press, 2010.

Shreveport Times: "Is the Municipal Really Haunted," http://web.archive.org/web/20130616012427/http://www .shreveporttimes.com/article/20130612/NEWS01/306110047

You can also check out videos about the haunting on YouTube, including testimony from witnesses of the ghostly activity. https://www.youtube.com/watch?v=yJzf4pk2D64

MEMORIAL HALL

Basehor Sentinel: "Ghost Tour Group Sets Its Sights on Memorial Hall Tour," http://www.basehorinfo.com/news/2009 /oct/08/ghost-tour-group-sets-its-sights-memorial-hall-tou/

Patsy Cline Discography: "Last Concert—March 3, 1963," http://patsyclinediscography.com/march3.php

THE BIJOU

Basehorinfo.com: "Ghost Tour Group Sets Its Sights—Memorial Hall Tour," http://www.basehorinfo.com/news/2009/oct/08 /ghost-tour-group-sets-its-sights-memorial-hall-tou/

Bijou Theatre History, http://www.knoxbijou.com/About-Us /bijou-theatre-history

Ghosts and Spirits of Tennesse, John Norris Broan, archived
here: https://web.archive.org/web/20140323070814/http://
www.johnnorrisbrown.com/paranormal-tn/bijou/index.htm

PARAMOUNT ART CENTER

Theresa's Haunted History of the Tri-State Haunting: "Billy Ray
Cyrus Meets a Ghost… At the Paramount Arts Center in
Ashland, Ky," http://theresashauntedhistoryofthetri-state
.blogspot.com/2011/05/billy-ray-cyrus-meets-ghostat
-paramount.html

Paramount Arts Center, http://paramountartscenter.com
/history-mission/

BOBBY MACKEY'S MUSIC WORLD

About.com: "The Ghosts of Bobby Mackey's Nightclub," http://
paranormal.about.com/od/hauntedplaces/a/aa031207.htm

Doubtful News: "Haunted history of Bobby Mackey's Music
World fails to stand up to scrutiny," http://doubtfulnews
.com/2015/04/haunted-history-of-bobby-mackeys-music
-world-fails-to-stand-up-to-scrutiny/

Haunted Houses: Bobby Mackey's Music World, http://www
.hauntedhouses.com/states/ky/bobby_mackeys.htm

Hensley, Douglas. *Hell's Gate: Terror at Bobby Mackey's Music
World.* Outskirts Press, 2005.

Smith, Dan. *Ghosts of Bobby Mackey's Music World.* Charleston,
SC: History Press, 2013.

As noted in the text, some information based on personal interviews with paranormal investigators who conduct tours of the premises.

A TOAST TO NASHVILLE'S GHOSTS

Marsh, Donna, Jeff Morris, and Garett Merk. *Haunted Nashville Handbook (America's Haunted Road Trip)*. Cincinnati, OH: Clerisy Press, 2011.

What-When-How.com: "Haunted Places, Tootsies," http://what -when-how.com/haunted-places/tootsie%E2%80%99s -orchid-lounge-nashville-tennessee-haunted-place/

MUSEUM CLUB

Legends of America: "Haunted Museum Club in Flagstaff," http://www.legendsofamerica.com/az-museumclub.html

CAPITOL RECORDS

Haunted Houses: "Capitol Records," http://www.hauntedhouses .com/states/tn/capitol_records.htm

Ghost Traveller: Tennessee, http://www.ghosttraveller.com /tennessee.htm

Coleman, Christopher K. *Ghosts and Haunts of Tennessee*. Winston-Salem, NC: John F. Blair, 2011.

RCA STUDIOS

Coleman, Christopher K. *Ghosts and Haunts of Tennessee*. Winston-Salem, NC: John F. Blair, 2011.

Real Haunted Places: "Nashville, TN - RCA Studio B," http://
    realhauntedplaces.blogspot.com/2011/10/nashville-tn
    -rca-studio-b.html

BENNETT HOUSE (BAGBEY HOUSE)

Bagbey House: Bennett Family Lineage, https://web.archive.org
    /web/20160314231614/http://bagbeyhouse.com/index.php
    /about/bennett-family-lineage

RECORD SHOPS THAT ARE HAUNTED HOT SPOTS

Marsh, Donna, Jeff Morris, and Garett Merk. *Haunted Nashville
    Handbook (America's Haunted Road Trip)*. Cincinnati, OH:
    Clerisy Press, 2011.

FREAKY FREQUENCIES

Salem-News, "Haunted Oregon Radio Station Still Restless
    Decades Later," http://www.salem-news.com/articles
    /november262012/oregon-ghosts-tk.php
WTXL website, "Big Moose's New Ghost Friend," http://www
    .wtxl.com/news/hot-on-the-web-big-moose-s-new-ghost
    -friend/article_f948b6b6-93d7-11e3-aeaf-001a4bcf6878.html

BIG CEDAR LODGE

Big Cedar Lodge website, http://www.big-cedar.com/Page/The
    -Legend-of-Buzzard-Bar.aspx

Explore Southern History: "The Ghost of Big Cedar Resort—
Branson, Missouri," http://www.exploresouthernhistory.com
/bigcedarghost.html

"Haunted Hotel rooms with a BOO!," by NBC Travel Editor
Peter Greenberg, accessed via http://www.angelfire.com/ri
/spookycat/travelhaunts.html

WALKING HORSE HOTEL

Walking Horse Hotel: Haunted Hotel, http://web.archive.org
/web/20140505023913/http://walkinghorsehotel.com
/haunted-hotel

THE STOCKYARDS HOTEL

Brown, Alan. *The Big Book of Texas Ghost Stories*. Mechanics-
burg, PA: Stackpole Books, 2012.

Cook, Rita. *Haunted Fort Worth*. Charleston, SC: History Press,
2011.

http://www.tripadvisor.com/ShowUserReviews-g55857
-d114952-r73831843-Stockyards_Hotel-Fort_Worth_Texas.
html

MAISON DE VILLE

Maison de Ville, http://www.maisondeville.com/

Ghosts of Louisiana: "Maison de Ville," http://www.ghostsof
louisiana.com/MDV.html

THE OZARK SPOOK LIGHTS

Mysterious Universe: "The Missouri Spook Light," http://mysteriousuniverse.org/2013/05/the-missouri-spook -light/

Prosser, Lee. *Branson Hauntings*. Atglen, PA: Schiffer Publishing, 2010.

BROWN MOUNTAIN LIGHTS

Brown Mountain Lights, www.brownmountainlights.com

One of the best resources available for this phenomena is available on the web as a free pdf. *Brown Mountain Lights Viewing Guide* by Joseph P. Warren accessed via http://shadowboxent .brinkster.net/bml%20viewing%20guide_9-16-13.pdf

FIDDLER'S ROCK

Ghosts of the Prairie: "Fiddler's Rock," http://www.prairie ghosts.com/fiddler.html

The Moonlit Road: "The Ghost of Fiddler's Rock," http:// themoonlitroad.com/the-ghost-of-fiddlers-rock/

FOLSOM PRISON

The Examiner, "Arizona Ghost Hunter Travels: Thanksgiving at Folsom Prison," http://www.examiner.com/article/arizona -ghost-hunter-travels-thanksgiving-at-folsom-prison?sms _ss=digg&at_xt=4ce991b643c66fb8%2C0

Folsom Telegraph, "Ghostly Tales Haunt Historic Folsom Prison," http://foamcage.com/arizona-ghost-hunter-travels -thanksgiving-at-folsom-prison/

WITCH DANCE AND LYRIC THEATER

Ghost Stories: "Lyric Theater," http://paranormalstories
    .blogspot.com/2010/09/lyric-theater.html

Northeast Mississippi Daily Journal, "TCT to Open Haunted
    Theatre on Friday," http://djournal.com/news/tct-to-open
    -haunted-theatre-on-friday/

Phantoms and Monsters: "Ghosts of Tupelo, Mississippi," http://
    www.phantomsandmonsters.com/2010/06/ghosts-of-tupelo
    -mississippi.html

PRESTON CASTLE

Ghost Stories, "Preston Castle," http://paranormalstories
    .blogspot.com/2009/06/preston-castle.html

Unexplained Mysteries: "My Preston Castle Ghost Story," http://
    www.unexplained-mysteries.com/column.php?id=187971

HAUNTED JUKEBOXES

Burger One website, http://www.burgerone.com/country
    -restaurant-clarendon/ghost-story.html

Clarendon Hills Historical Society: "Country House Ghost,"
    http://clarendonhillshistory.org/clarendon-hills-history
    /country-house-ghost/

Ghost Adventures websites and episode, Season 1, episode 1,
    http://ghostadventures.wikia.com/wiki/Bobby_Mackey's
    _Music_World_(episode)

Hensley, Douglas. *Hell's Gate: Terror at Bobby Mackey's Music World*. Outskirts Press, 2005.

Swayne, Matthew. *Haunted Rock and Roll*. Woodbury, MN: Llewellyn, 2013.

HAUNTED TOUR BUS

You can read more about Whisperin' Bill Anderson's paranormal tour at the following blogs. A few of the sites still have videos that document the supposed run-ins with the ghost.

The Boot, http://theboot.com/bill-anderson-tour-2010

That Nashville Sound Blog, http://thatnashvillesound.blogspot .com/2010/03/bill-anderson-dealing-with-haunted-tour.html

EPILOGUE

CSICOP: Elvis Lives!, http://www.csicop.org/sb/show/elvis _lives_investigating_the_legends_and_phenomena/

TO WRITE TO THE AUTHOR

If you wish to contact the author or would like more information about this book, please write to the author in care of Llewellyn Worldwide Ltd. and we will forward your request. Both the author and publisher appreciate hearing from you and learning of your enjoyment of this book and how it has helped you. Llewellyn Worldwide Ltd. cannot guarantee that every letter written to the author can be answered, but all will be forwarded. Please write to:

Matthew L. Swayne
⁒ Llewellyn Worldwide
2143 Wooddale Drive
Woodbury, MN 55125-2989

Please enclose a self-addressed stamped envelope for reply,
or $1.00 to cover costs. If outside the U.S.A., enclose
an international postal reply coupon.

Many of Llewellyn's authors have websites with additional information and resources. For more information, please visit our website at http://www.llewellyn.com

GET MORE AT LLEWELLYN.COM

Visit us online to browse hundreds of our books and decks, plus sign up to receive our e-newsletters and exclusive online offers.

- **Free tarot readings** • **Spell-a-Day** • **Moon phases**
- **Recipes, spells, and tips** • **Blogs** • **Encyclopedia**
- **Author interviews, articles, and upcoming events**

GET SOCIAL WITH LLEWELLYN

Find us on
Facebook

www.Facebook.com/LlewellynBooks

Follow us on

www.Twitter.com/Llewellynbooks

GET BOOKS AT LLEWELLYN

LLEWELLYN ORDERING INFORMATION

Order online: Visit our website at www.llewellyn.com to select your books and place an order on our secure server.

Order by phone:
- Call toll free within the U.S. at 1-877-NEW-WRLD (1-877-639-9753)
- Call toll free within Canada at 1-866-NEW-WRLD (1-866-639-9753)
- We accept VISA, MasterCard, American Express and Discover

Order by mail:
Send the full price of your order (MN residents add 6.875% sales tax) in U.S. funds, plus postage and handling to: Llewellyn Worldwide, 2143 Wooddale Drive Woodbury, MN 55125-2989

POSTAGE AND HANDLING

STANDARD (U.S. & Canada):
(Please allow 12 business days)
$30.00 and under, add $4.00.
$30.01 and over, FREE SHIPPING.

INTERNATIONAL ORDERS:
$16.00 for one book, plus $3.00 for each additional book.

Visit us online for more shipping options. Prices subject to change.

FREE CATALOG!

To order, call
1-877-
NEW-WRLD
ext. 8236
or visit our
website